10:37

By
Jacqueline Druga

10:37
By Jacqueline Druga
Copyright 2017 by Jacqueline Druga

This is a work of fiction. Names, characters, places and incidents are either the product of the author's imagination or are used fictitiously, and any resemblance to any person or persons, living or dead, events or locales is entirely coincidental.

Thank you to Paula Gibson and Kira for your help and encouragement on this one.

Cover Art by Christian Bentulan
www.coversbychristian.com

This book is dedicated to the memory of Linda Korman, a devoted reader of all my books.

ONE – THE FALL

"Don't chew on your eraser, Dawson."

That was the last thing Dawson Montgomery heard, or something like that. It was a bit more, his third grade teacher never gave just a warning, she didn't stop there, and it wasn't that simple. It was always a warning, followed by the why and then the consequences.

"Don't chew on your eraser, Dawson, you'll swallow it and choke. Then what? The whole class will have to stop just because you have a fidget problem."

He never liked when she did that, and it always seemed as if she did that to him a lot. Singled him out, drawing attention to him, and embarrassing him.

Dawson embarrassed easily, especially in school, he didn't know why. Maybe because he had a hard time with things. Math was a breeze, but reading and answering questions about what he read didn't come fast, or easy. He had to think. That meant hand to his forehead causing his dark blonde hair to stick straight up, all while biting on his pencil.

That was what he did that morning while doing his seat work. He read the story, it was dumb. However, Dawson wasn't dumb, he just didn't answer correctly when it came to things he didn't like. He was convinced had the story been about wrestling or monsters, he'd get every answer right.

Not when it came to a story about a boy named Sam who had to help his farmer friend carry a pail of water. Dawson didn't care much for the story when he read it and answering the questions was even harder when the teacher yelled at him every fifteen seconds.

What Dawson wanted to do was tell her to stop, but that meant sitting out recess.

Recess.

He wasn't really great at telling time, but he knew once that big hand swung up to the twelve, the bell would ring and it was lunch.

He couldn't wait.

Dawson looked up to the clock. It was half way there, little hand on the eleven, big hand just passed the six.

"Dawson, don't bite that ..."

She scared him. He was concentrating, and when she did that, he bit the erased clean off into his mouth.

Instinct caused him to immediately spit it out, but he wondered if he actually did. All of the sudden, Dawson couldn't breathe. His throat closed up as if something was in there, his skin felt on fire, and everything went blurry around him. Every inhale was impossible. No air could get into his lungs.

There was no noise, Dawson couldn't move. He couldn't scream for help. It was the one time he wanted his teacher's attention. She didn't seem to notice. Heart racing out of control, Dawson didn't have time to panic, everything went black and his head dropped to the desk.

<><><><>

At first, Morgan Welsh tried to be calm and rational, but as soon as she heard Craig's voice on the speaker phone, she lost it ... again.

"Fuck you. I mean it, fuck you, you're such a fucking asshole," she verbally hit him.

"Yeah, that's nice, Morg. Real nice. You done?" Craig asked. "No hello first, before you bitch me out?'

"No."

"Then why call?"

"What am I going to do, text it to you?" she asked.

"That's what most people do."

"I fucking hate you. "

"Jesus, Morgan."

Morgan hated that Craig remained calm, unrattled. She was angry, beyond that actually. Morgan was an ever changing wheel of emotions. Happy, sad, angry, bitter... it wasn't anything medical, it was all marriage related. It was out of her control, and she hated when anything was out of her control. Her job and entire life was under her thumb. From what she did in the workplace to how she paid the bills ... Morgan had it intact, until the day she grabbed Craig's phone by mistake and learned her marriage was the one thing she didn't have a realistic grasp on.

How it slipped from her, she didn't know.

Married life was done, suddenly Morgan was thrust into a different way of living and she, like many others, strongly disliked change.

"What do you want today, Morgan? Aren't you supposed to be at work? Oh, wait, are you late again? The every punctual, never make a mistake Morgan, is screwing up her job?'

"It's your fault," she argued.

"Okay, I'm game. How is your being late my fault?"

"I went to check the bank account. You're spending our money ..."

"My money."

"Our money!" she blasted. "While it is a joint account, while we are still married, it is our money and you're spending it on her."

"I'm not spending it on her."

"You're lying again."

"I'm not lying. I'm spending it on me so I can enjoy spending time with her. Does it make you feel better?"

Morgan hated the way she felt, enraged. Why couldn't Craig just be happy with her, why did he have to find someone else? While she lived under a fantasy that all was well in the Welsh marriage, Craig had been seeing a woman in the next county.

"The only thing that will make me feel better," Morgan said. "Is if you drop dead."

The moment she said that and did the power house 'end call' she felt her chest collapse and all air escape her.

Suddenly every pumping ounce of her blood burned as it ran rapidly through her veins.

Was it a panic attack, heart attack? It couldn't be. Morgan had never had one, yet she was choking. She couldn't take air in, or let it out.

Her eyes widened, and with the instant thought to hit the brakes or pull over, she instinctively grabbed for her own throat. Her hands were off the wheel a split second when she felt the hard jolt and bang as a car slammed into the passenger door. It spun her vehicle into the next lane facing the opposite direction.

Even in her duress she was still semi aware enough to see she was on a one way collision course with a truck speeding her way. Losing consciousness, Morgan gripped the wheel and turned it. She traded one impact for another. She was like a billiard ball bouncing from one car to another. Morgan never felt it though, her head dropped to the steering wheel just as she entered the vehicular game of pool.

◇◇◇◇

It didn't even make sense, Judd Bryant thought. He understood his producer wanted an awesome looking music video, however he was still scratching his head over what the heck a construction site had to do with his newest song. Not to mention he was afraid of heights and now they wanted him on the ninth floor of a shell of a building, strumming his guitar and singing, "*You dropped me like a bad habit.*" It was dumb. He just didn't get it. No one really watched music videos anymore unless they had some sort of hook. They didn't do a music video the year before and his song "Craving Carrot Cake and Karen' stayed at number one in the country charts for eight weeks

"You'll take the crew elevator up," his manager, Ben said. "Stand on the ledge and just strum and sing"

"No, absolutely not," Judd told him. "Get a stunt double."

"Judd, chicks love a guy who does his own stunts."

"Which is why they call them doubles, so no one knows"

"'Man you're sad. What happened to the fearless country boy?" Ben asked.

"Fearless?" Judd laughed. "I may be country, but I have never been fearless. Ever. I don't even swim. Seriously Ben, this is insane. Even the camera guy has a stunt double."

"That's called a camera drone."

"Yeah, he's not up there filming, even he can see it's insane."

"It's perfectly safe. If you want, I'll come up there with you and stay out of the shot."

"You'll balance on the beam with me?" Judd asked.

"There's not any balancing, the entire floor is finished up there."

Judd placed his hands on his hips and looked up to the structure. It wasn't his thing, it really wasn't. He didn't like getting in front of a camera. An audience was different, he was confident playing guitar. When it came to heights he wasn't. Despite his celebrity status, Judd was a man of simple means. He didn't like conflict and he hated letting people down. After a few minutes of staring up and some debating, he figured what would it hurt.

"Okay, fine, but if I fall..."

"You'll sell a million records."

"Asshole!"

"Grab your guitar big guy, these workers don't have all day to wait for us to get done." Ben gave a hand signal to the director that all was good.

"I'm pretty sure they're fine with just standing around," Judd lifted his guitar, paused for a second, then called for Ben. "Wait.

"What?" Ben asked.

"Here." Judd handed Ben a bottle of water.

"I'm not thirsty."

"No, I need you to spill it behind me."

"What?" Ben laughed the word.

"Spill it behind me. It's good luck."

"Spilling water behind you is good luck?"

"It's an age old Serbian custom."

"You're not Serbian."

"I'm pretty sure with the way the world is a melting pot, we all have a little Serbian in us."

"I doubt that."

"I do," said Judd. "Two percent. I did one of those DNA things. So, please."

Ben grunted and took the water. "You know it's not spilling, it's pouring."

"It's okay," Judd said.

Disgruntled, Ben walked behind Judd and poured some water. 'There." He handed him the bottle. "Feel better?'

"Much. Want me to put some behind you?"

"No. I'm fine. I don't believe in superstitions." Ben walked away.

A construction worker waited to take them up using the temporary elevator on the outside of the structure. Judd kept thinking about how if he fell, there was no surviving it.

Once up the floor, Judd didn't feel so bad, even after the elevator lowered. The building was only missing walls.

He placed his guitar on, and out of habit, strummed it a few times.

"Okay," the director yelled through the megaphone. "Wait for my call. You should be able to hear the music, strum along, I only need a few good shots."

Judd gave a thumbs up. Then noticed Ben walking near the edge. "Get back."

"I'm fine. It's not as high as I thought."

"It's high enough. Now get back. You're in the shot anyhow."

"I'm ..." Ben grew silent.

With his back to Judd, Ben didn't move, then his hands shot up and Judd watched his elbows flap.

"You trying to be a bird."

Ben didn't answer. "Ben? You Okay?"

He turned slightly to face Judd. Ben's face was blue and his hands clasped his throat. He made eye contact with Judd, then tipped to his left and fell over the edge.

"Ben!" Judd charged forth, stopping just at the edge. "Someone call 911!" For a split second, Judd believed he had seen the worst thing in his life. In a panic, he peered over the edge, not only did he see Ben, but the director and then the body of a construction worker fell from above him. It fell straight down, fast and lifeless, then another fell.

Was he having a nightmare? What was happening? Sounds of metal against metal, car crashes, bang and booms rang out all around him.

Judd's heart raced out of control and he opened his mouth to scream, nothing came out. He couldn't breathe and it wasn't from lack of air. It was like in a second the world ended, and he was the only one still standing.

TWO – WAKE

Gasp!

The air entered Dawson's lungs and, head still on the desk, he opened his eyes with the large breath that revived him. He was confused, didn't know what was happening. He remembered choking or not being able to breathe and that was it. Things were blurry. He expected to be scolded by the teacher for falling asleep. He was afraid to lift his head. Would she believe he fell to the desk and it wasn't in his control? Even if she did believe he choked, she'd then yell at him.

Dawson had to face the music.

He sat up.

The only sound in the room was the ticking of the second hand on the clock. Slowly he looked around. What was going on? His classmates all had their heads laying on their desks, he didn't even see his teacher. Slowly he stood up. It was a prank, he thought. They were pranking him because he fell asleep.

"Guys," he said. "Guys it's not funny. You can stop."

No one moved. The class room was silent.

"It's not funny!" He shouted. His stomach twitched and his hands shook, he was scared. Extending a hand he reached out to Melinda. Her head was down, eyes open and she had a blue look to her.

How did she do that? How did she look like that?

Dawson was young, he never claimed to be smart, but he knew the second he touched Mclinda that she wasn't joking.

Her skin was cold and she didn't move.

In a panic, he kept pushing her. "Wake up," he said. "Wake up." He moved her harder, yet she didn't respond.

Dawson didn't stop, he shook and shook her until a frightening reality hit him. Melinda wouldn't wake up and neither would anyone else in his classroom.

He spun around to race from the classroom and he saw the blood on the floor. A huge puddle seeped out from the side of the teacher's desk.

When he stepped closer, that was when he saw her

His teacher. She lay on the floor, her color was like Melinda's and a pool of blood not only encircled her head but flowed out like a river.

Knowing he had to get someone, Billy fled the room screaming, "Help."

He raced out of the class room screaming, then a thought hit him. What if someone did it? He heard the news, he knew people did bad things like that at school. With that thought, Dawson quit screaming. He stopped running and moved quietly. When he did, he passed another class. His head slowly turned to his right and he saw the same thing. Everyone in that classroom was the same way.

He picked up his pace trying not to slam his feet on the floor. It didn't matter, the halls were so quiet, every move he made echoed. The office wasn't far, at the end of the hall actually. He had to let the principal know. She would help.

When he was near enough, he peeked to make sure he didn't see any bad guys and he shot full speed around the bend into the office.

Dawson didn't even cry for help. He saw Miss Molly the secretary with her head on her desk and the principal's legs extended out of a doorway behind her.

His little heart beat so fast and his entire being was consumed with a fear that no adult could ever experience. Tears formed in his eyes and then fell rapidly down his cheeks.

Scared, but knowing he had to try, Dawson reached for the phone and dialed 911.

It rang and rang, no one answered.

He thought about hiding, waiting for help to get there, but he was afraid the bad person was still inside.

After peeking out of the office, he raced as fast as his legs would carry him, down the hall and out the double front doors.

As soon as he blasted outside, he knew.

In front of the school, two cars were crashed and the sound of their still running motors were the only noise. A man and his dog lay on the sidewalk, not moving.

It wasn't just his class or his school, it was everywhere and in his confused and frightened state, Dawson did what any child would do at that moment. Emotions took over and he sat down on the curb and sobbed.

<><><><>

Morgan floated. At least she felt as if she did. Flashes of light came at her as if she were sailing through space. She moved quickly and was even conscious about it. After feeling the last impact, she was lucid and aware.

"This is peace," she thought. *"I am at peace. Thank God."*

She figured her anxiety attack or even coronary, was the reason for the car crash. She hoped no one else was hurt or killed. As she floated she didn't even know why she was angry in the first place, why she was upset? It didn't matter. She felt free and at ease.

"If this is death, then I am good with it."

She didn't feel pain, none at all. Before the accident, something caused her to ache all over, something emotional, but that was gone.

Morgan was flying.

The lights grew brighter and she believed, any second, she would see her mother, her father and her sister.

All waiting on the other side. Waiting to greet her. She moved even faster, then suddenly something changed, something was different.

A pressure filled her ears and in an instant the bright lights left, it all turned dark and a sharp pain hit her chest. With that pain, her eyes opened and she sat back quickly with a wheezing breath that was deep and loud.

Morgan would have sworn someone hit her with a defibrillator had she not been alone, her face inches from a bloody and deflated air bag.

A car horn blasted continuously, but it wasn't hers. It was in the distance. She tried to move, but even moving an inch, caused sharp pains everywhere. Her head especially throbbed and there was something heavy and wet on her eyes, causing her vision to be blurry. Slowly she brought up her right hand. Her entire arm shook as she brought her fingers across her eyes.

Blood.

It was blood in her eyes. It had to be from her head.

Morgan tired breathing, when she did, she felt it in her ribs. They ached horribly.

Something was broken, but what.

There were no sirens, nothing. With her other hand she reached for the door, but couldn't even grip the handle. She was too weak.

Another inhale, and Morgan drew in enough breath to squeak out a barely audible. "Help."

That wasn't going to work, no one would hear her.

She tried again, this time louder. "Help." Her shoulders bounced with emotions and after one more attempt to scream out, Morgan gave up.

The pain was too much and she started to cry.

Just as she lowered her head back down to the steering wheel, her driver's door flung open.

"You're alive," he said.

Morgan whimpered and only had enough strength to turn her head. "Yes," she peeped out.

"I got you," he said. "Hold on. It might hurt when I get you out. You're alive. Thank God."

He leaned into her. She didn't see much of this man, only a brief glimpse of his darker skin and the blue of his shirt as he reached his arms to her.

When he lifted her, it hurt, but she was grateful. A brief glimpse of the police badge on his chest, and Morgan collapsed against his chest.

She was saved.

Everything would be all right.

<><><><>

It wasn't Judd's first disaster rodeo, that was the reason he was able to keep his calm.

He blamed himself. Ever since he was a kid it was like he was a magnet for trouble, but it was worse as he grew older.

There was the one and only earthquake to cause massive damage in Kansas City, he was supposed to play that night. He stumbled out of the rubble of his hotel to massive casualties everywhere. He rolled up his sleeves and helped.

The F-5 that struck outside of Oklahoma City ... he was playing. He was whisked from the stage moments before the stage ... was whisked away.

There were many others. Judd just happened to be there.

For a while the press had a field day with his reputation and people created memes.

'Tsunami warning? If Judd Bryant is in town, you should leave.'

He had seen a lot, been through a lot, but never anything like what he was now experiencing.

Everyone was dead.

The electricity was still going yet he opted not to take the service elevator. His very first thought was a terror attack, some sort of mega chemical weapon was unleashed on Akron, Ohio. Although he couldn't figure out who would want to hurt Akron.

It was the only thing that made sense though.

An attack. Smoke rose to the sky and there were fires everywhere.

Judd knew he had to find a way to get out of the city. A place he didn't know, he was there for a concert. The music video was a last minute thing, decided on when they were in Lexington just one week earlier.

He didn't have any knowledge of Akron, just that he was in a construction site not far from a suburb. He took the stairs from the ninth floor, paused by Ben's body to pay respects, then lifted his phone. He expected choppers or planes to fly over, but they didn't.

Obviously the area was quarantined, especially if it was a weapon.

He had a signal and instinctively called 911. There was no answer and he went on the internet. The news site didn't mention anything and he immediately logged onto social media.

Again, nothing there.

There was no way, in his mind, that the attack went further than Akron.

So he began to walk the neighborhood.

Not far from the site, was a main roadway. It was a mess, cars were smashed into each other, people slumped over the steering wheels, others had collapsed on the sidewalk.

"Keep it together," he told himself. Judd had a freak out moment when he watched Ben fall, then the others. He lost it. Then reality hit him that there was nothing he could do, but be what he was ... a survivor.

He called out as he walked, asking for anyone to answer, no one did.

Two blocks into his journey, the main road crossed through a residential area. He walked through the parking lot of a convenience store gas station. Cars were at the pumps, people lay by their vehicles, some held the nozzles, as if they grabbed them in their final moments of life, pulling on the handles, toppling. Another car was pressed against a pump, the driver against the wheel, the vehicle hit the pump with enough force to spring a leak. A stream of gasoline flowed into the street.

Seeing the button for the emergency shutoff, Judd ran over and pushed it. He couldn't do anything about the gas already spilled but he felt like he had done something.

There was a bar next to the gas station and a lone pick-up truck was parked there. He knew it was early, but the bar was his best chance for a television.

He approached the single oak door with the lunch special notice and opened it.

"Hello!" He hollered as he stepped in. "Anyone here?"

There wasn't anyone that he could see, at least at the tables, the bar, or on the floor. The lights were low, but a case of beer was on top of the bar and next to that, the register drawer.

Someone was getting ready to open it.

The television was in the corner up high and Judd walked behind the bar to look for a remote.

Behind the bar was a body. Judd deducted that was probably the bartender. Trying not to look, Judd searched around the register and found the remote in a basket with pens. He lifted it and aimed it at the television, turning it on.

Some old movie played and Judd switched the channels until he hit a news station. At that instant, he froze. There was no ticker tape rolling across the bottom telling of breaking news.

It was a single image. The camera angle was skewed some and everything was off center. Clearly it was a newsroom, the backdrop wall of televisions played static, while the anchorman slumped lifeless over the desk.

Right there and then, Judd knew. He was ready to learn about the attack, ready to know how bad it was, at least he thought he was until he saw that. It wasn't just Akron, it was everywhere. For that revelation, Judd was not prepared.

THREE – POOR THING

Dawson was so overcome with emotions, both fear and sadness that he passed out on the sidewalk in front of the school. Before he did, he kept thinking that his parents were at work and would hear about the school and come get him. He didn't want to leave or go running off somewhere, then they wouldn't find him.

Like many boys his age, he had an imagination, but Dawson always took his imagination one step further. He was controlled by it at times, his extensive day dreams and trips to his fantasy imaginations were often the cause of many parent teacher conferences.

"Save it for after school," his teacher would tell him.

Dawson couldn't control it.

If he saw a bird, suddenly his mind went elsewhere.

He had day dreams about being a hero, fighting Professor Fry, the evil bad guy who tried to destroy the world. In his mind, Professor Fry was always the one and only man cafeteria worker. He was scary, the perfect bad guy to defeat.

Even in all his wildest fantasy scenarios never did Dawson envision one like he just witnessed.

He wished this time was one of those times he was told that he 'lived in a made up world', then he could shake his head, focus and make it go away.

It wasn't.

All his friends and teachers were dead.

Professor Fry didn't do it. Someone did.

He didn't dream when he fell asleep, but he woke up to a loud whistle. A whirling sound that grew louder and louder.

Dawson jumped, grabbing his ears. The sound was so loud it hurt. He looked up to see a plane shooting like a missile above his head. It flew low and on its side, so close Dawson swore he could touch it. It wasn't the engines that made a noise, it was the plane cutting through the air.

A few seconds later, not only was it gone, it crashed somewhere. The ground shook violently and a huge fireball erupted in the sky.

He screamed and turned to run back into the school, when he saw smoke billowing up from the far end by the gym. He didn't see any flames, but he knew there had to be a fire.

Knowing he couldn't stay there, Dawson had one option, which was to go home. He had never walked to school. His father always drove him and his mother picked him up. He knew where he lived, he just had to remember how to get there. That would probably be the second place his parents would go.

He wanted to go back in and get his book bag, but he was smart enough not to run into a building that was on fire.

After looking both ways, Dawson crossed the street and headed in the direction of his home.

It was a blessing and a curse that Dawson loved horror films, more so that his parents let him watch scary things. Scary things within reason. Then again, they didn't know half the stuff he watched because he would use his tablet and watch videos on line. After his father yelled at him once for watching 'inappropriate' videos, he just used his mother's account. No one checked that.

The videos made him brave and smart and also caused his imagination to take off.

He walked fast, looking for landmarks, and when he passed by and saw the tobacco store, the one his father said didn't really sell tobacco, he knew he had taken the long way home, but he also knew where to go.

Dawson hadn't seen a person at all, nor did he hear a dog or bird. He tried not to look at anything, the car crashes, or bodies on the street. He focused ahead, watching the black smoke from the plane crash as it darkened the sky.

He stayed low and out of sight, keeping a keen eye out. He remembered the videos and movies and wasn't ruling out that all those bodies on the sidewalk would stand up, walk and want to eat him.

Aim for the head.

That would be easy if Dawson was taller, but he wasn't. He was pretty short for his age, the smallest kid in his class. His best defense against the walking dead was to run and hide.

He hoped it was just a bad man or bad people that made it happen.

Finally, Dawson made it to his street and he ran all the way home. Neither parent's car was in the driveway. He didn't expect that. They were working.

He knew to go to the basement door near the garage, a key was there. It took him awhile fumbling and he figured out which way to turn it. It was when he opened the door that he finally noticed it. The sound of a lawn mower. Hearing a mower was such a common thing it didn't register, until he thought about it.

Someone was mowing the lawn.

Someone was alive.

He pulled the door closed and stepped out into the driveway, listening.

It came from his left and his eyes widened.

Mr. Westerman, a grandfatherly man who didn't work anymore. He was always mowing his lawn. Pushing the old mower back and forth, up the small hill, even if the yard didn't need cut. He lived two doors away and Dawson took off in that direction.

"Mr. Westerman!" Dawson shouted as he ran. "Mr. Westerman."

The lawn mower kept going. A steady buzz.

Sure enough, it was coming from behind Mr. Westerman's house and Dawson sprinted back to his house.

Once inside, he locked the door. In fact, he locked all the doors. He had to remember to be quiet. Just in case. If the dead got up, they'd hear him cry and scream, and then find him.

They didn't have a house phone and Dawson wasn't old enough for a cell, so he couldn't call his mom or dad, or even call for help. He thought about going to the neighbors, but didn't want to see if they were dead.

On the way through the basement family room, he paused and looked at the family picture above the fireplace. The one where they tried fishing, when none of them knew how to fish. His mom loved that picture and she looked pretty in it. Her hair was the same color as his, everyone always said that. Lighter when the sun hit it, but he looked like his dad, built like him, too. Not real tall, pretty thin everywhere but in the middle. They used to jiggle their bellies at the same time to music. It was fun. When he saw that picture, Dawson got sad again.

He hoped his mom and dad were safe. He needed his parents to be alright. Something inside of him feared they weren't.

He couldn't think that way. He rushed up the stairs and called out, just in case they walked home like him. There was no answer and Dawson was afraid to look around.

In fact, he was scared of his own home and he knew what he had to do.

He opened the fridge, grabbed drink boxes, the bag of string cheese, two of those lunch things, and chips. Arms loaded, he retreated to his room and locked the door and window.

He moved the toy box in front of the door, grabbed his tablet, plugged it in and laid on his bed.

There he would stay until his parents got him. He'd watch videos, all day and all night if he had to. It would keep him busy, take his mind away and keep him from crying and getting too scared.

Dawson did that, losing track of time, far into the night until he fell fast asleep.

FOUR – WHO ARE YOU

The woman was hurt, pretty badly too. Ross Howard wasn't at a loss on how to help the woman he pulled from the car, he just didn't know where to start. Although he never thought about leaving her hair stuck to her face. It acted like a coagulant and the moment he pulled it aside to clean her wounds, the gash on her head bled profusely. It didn't want to stop.

He didn't think anything was broken, though he couldn't be sure. He had to wait until she regained consciousness, if she ever did, to find out where it hurt. Until then, he did what he could. He had to, he needed her to survive

She was alive and he intended to keep her that way.

Ross was pretty sure there weren't any doctors or medical personnel, at least not close by.

He was a realist.

Something happened, something big happened and his mind spun with trying to figure out exactly what it was.

In his sixteen years on the police force, Ross swore he had seen it all. Obviously, he hadn't.

It was a pretty uneventful day up until ten minutes before everything just died. An unusual occurrence for the Pittsburgh area. Ross was happy about that, he had issued three traffic citations and a warning, he planned to go out to dinner with his wife for their anniversary, even though it was still three days away. He stopped by Station Square to make a reservation and was on his way down the Boulevard when he and his partner received the call about a robbery in progress at a news shop. There wasn't any money to be gained there, everyone knew that. Small time, it had to be some kids trying to get drug money.

They pulled over with sirens blaring and hadn't even had time to draw their weapons when the first shot sailed through the glass door, killing his partner instantly.

"Officer down," Ross called out. "Need ..."

Both gunman came from the store, one used an older woman as a human shield. His arm around her neck and a gun to her head.

"Back up or I'll shoot her," the young man said. "I mean it."

Ross knew he did, but he didn't have time to react.

It happened. Ross saw it first.

For a second everything rippled before his eyes. Like when heat rises off a barbecue, distorting everything with a wavy effect. Ross thought it was his blood pressure, after all his heart was racing out of control. Then his throat and nose burned out of control, which happened a moment before he lost his ability to take in air.

He tried, nothing would enter his lungs. It wasn't just him. The two assailants, the older woman were worse off. They turned blue before his eyes, dropping their guns, grabbing their throats before finally taking a lifeless nose dive to the pavement.

Was it because he was bigger? Ross didn't know, but he fought through it, and was grateful he did, had he lost consciousness he would have been killed when a car, full speed ahead, jumped the curb, ran over the two assailants then crashed through the window of the news shop.

He gasped as he was finally able to breathe, he did so in enough time to dive out of the way of another car.

Ross realized those on the street weren't the only ones keeling over, people in their cars were, too.

The Boulevard was a busy street and those who dropped on the sidewalk looked like roadkill when cars from the road just smashed over them.

He was, from what he could tell, the only person standing and he raced into the bank, nearly tripping over the bodies on the floor as he made his way to the far back wall near the vault.

He felt safe there from any wayward vehicles. At least he would see them coming.

It only took a minute for it all to stop.

When it did, Ross waited a few more minutes before heading outside.

Continuous car horns rang out along with hissing sounds from smashed cars. Vehicles were toppled over each other. So much was a mangled mess.

He walked to the street, placed his hands to his head and turned around. The wreckage was everywhere.

It was a chemical attack. It had to be. Something new, something he hadn't heard of. That's why he saw the ripple and felt the burn, that was the only thing that made sense. How did he survive it? He looked at the bodies on the ground, those in the cars, they were all blue. Asphyxiated blue.

Ross grabbed the radio and pressed the button. He made his call to the station, waited, hearing nothing.

"Come on," Ross beckoned, then tried again. Still nothing. "Anyone!" he shouted out. "Can anyone hear me?"

He heard the squeak of a car door and he looked up. Across the street, he watched a young man of maybe twenty stumble from a car.

"Thank God." Ross rushed over to him. "Son, hold on. You may be injured."

The young man turned around, a metal object protruded from his chest. His eyes met with Ross. "Help me." He pleaded.

Ross reached for him, but the young man fell to the ground. Immediately he lowered himself to the man and felt for a pulse, but the young man had died. It was something different for Ross to think about though as he didn't die from whatever happened.

If the young man had lived through it and if Ross beat it, then somebody else could, too. More than anything his first instinct was to get home to check his wife then go to the school and look for his girls. In the interim, he would listen and look for anyone else alive.

His best bet were the car accidents. They were severe, limbs scattered about the road, bodies ejected. On top of that, there was the frustration of the car horns. Not all that many, but enough to make hearing anything difficult.

He found one caused by a driver and by lifting the driver from the wheel silenced it.

Then he discovered another. Just as he cut that, he heard what he thought was a voice. He dismissed it as his imagination, until he heard it again. Ross moved frantically looking in each car until he saw her. He feared, she too, like the young man, died when her head fell to the steering wheel. But she opened her eyes when he opened the door.

Ross pulled her out and lifted her into his arms.

Looking left then right, Ross sought a safe place to take her to, place her down and help her until he could figure a way out of the city, or at least find a route not blocked with cars.

He spotted a law office on the corner, right across from the news shop. It wasn't far and he carried her there. The door was unlocked and he brought her inside.

He didn't see anyone and he laid her down on the couch in the reception area.

Calling out was futile, he knew that when he saw the receptionist on the floor behind the huge desk. He would deal with her body later, right then he wanted to make sure the woman from the car accident did not die.

"I'll be right back," he told her. She groaned, that was a good sign and he ran back outside. His police car was sandwiched between the news shop and a truck. The truck of the squad car was open from the collision. Perfect for Ross. He reached in, grabbed the first aid kit and a blanket.

He took the time to clean and bandage her wounds, hoping she had nothing internal. He covered her and tried to give her water, but she was unconscious.

"What am I doing?" he asked himself out loud. "I need to get home. I have to find my family."

He wanted to, even felt compelled to, but he also knew that leaving the woman to die, without trying to help, would be a huge mistake in the long run. He watched everyone just drop over. Since then, there were no sirens, no helicopters, and no military. Whatever hit was spread out pretty far.

Help wasn't on the way.

After about an hour of staring at the sleeping woman, not knowing anything about her, Ross sought out her car again, keeping an eye and ear out for anyone. The car horns had long since stopped blaring and the streets were finally silent.

Her phone was on the floor along with her purse, he grabbed them both and took them with him to the law office.

Once back, he rummaged through her purse and pulled out her wallet. He opened it, exposing her license.

"Now I have a name," he said and leaned close to her. "Wake up, Morgan. I need you to stay alive. Because right now, it looks like you and I are the only ones who are."

FIVE – BAD CHOICES

Judd didn't handle the apocalypse as well as he thought. In his mind he was taking it like a champ, but in reality he handled it more like a man on a suicidal mission, a man losing his mind.

It started in that bar, one drink turned into two, then he just grabbed a bottle and ate potato chips while staring at the dead news anchorman on the television set. It never changed, never went off the air.

It was hard to comprehend and hard to grieve an entire country. He was taking it in though, trying to process it. The person closest to him dropped off the side of an unfinished building right before his eyes. Beyond Ben, he had friends, no one that close. The life of a country music star always kept him from settling down with one person for very long. He had been dancing with fame since he was a skinny, scrawny teenager, performing on a reality show. Drumming up votes because his 'ma' had just died and it was just him, his father and brother living in a trailer. He skyrocketed after that, sort of the country music equivalent to a pop star. Although he never really went the fame and fortune route of the greats before him, work was steady, fans bought his records and he lived the dream.

He would have given it all up to have someone. He was grateful at that moment though, that he didn't have family or else Judd would have reacted differently.

His big brother had been in the Army and died serving his country. Judd's father, his biggest fan and best friend passed away just as, 'Craving Carrot Cake and Karen' hit number one.

Judd wandered around the neighborhood, looking for answers and for people.

He stopped at a church, it was empty and there were no bodies in there. He debated just hanging there, but when he heard the plane fall from the sky, he left. If a plane fell, then someone was alive to fly, at least for a while.

Then when he realized it was probably on autopilot until it ran out of fuel, hence why it only made a whistling sound. That caused him to look on his phone to see how many planes would be in the sky at one time.

If one fell, another one could do the same. It took him to a site that actually showed the planes in the air. He watched them disappear every few seconds.

By late afternoon, Judd was drunk. He found his way back to the construction site and sat in the rental car, his phone plugged into the charger.

He posted on social media.

'I'm alive and stuck in Akron, anyone else?'

"Did you know at any given time there are over two thousand planes in the sky?'

Random thoughts.

He even made a video, a drunken rambling message about being the last man on earth, stranded in Akron. Calling himself Charlton Heston in reference to the cult classic Omega Man. Then singing a song he wrote off the cuff called, *"Call me Mr. Heston."*

He was in a pathetic state and ready to leave Akron. By that time, it was late, he was hammered. Guided by bourbon balls, he made his way back up to the ninth floor of the building where he went to the air traffic website and watched until the final plane disappeared from that radar. After that, he passed out.

A pounding headache caused him to open his eyes and he was instantly awake when he realized how close to the edge he had rolled. How he didn't fall over and die, he didn't know.

The reality of what happened hit him when he saw Ben's body still on the ground below.

"Ah, man, Ben." Judd lowered his head.

Bing.

His eyes widened.

The tone rang out and it was from his phone. He looked around to where he put it and found it several feet from the edge.

It wasn't a text message. It was an alert. How many times had Ben told him to shut off his alerts on his video account.

"Nah," Judd told him. "The bing makes me know I'm still relevant. And I turn them off when I think it will go viral."

Judd had the alerts on, and he was glad he did.

He looked down to this phone. He had one new comment on his video.

He opened up the comment.

One comment, posted three minutes earlier from a woman named Rita Simms.

"I'm alive in Akron. I'm scared. Can you help me?"

"Oh, wow, yeah. Yeah." Judd said out loud. "Please be watching." He typed quickly. "Yes. Where are you?"

"I'm at my house."

"I can come there," Judd replied, his headache was secondary, the comment was like an immediate pain killer. He was thrilled, someone else was out there. There was hope. "What is the address. I think GPS still works."

A few seconds later, Rita replied with an address. Judd touched it and it brought up the 'maps'. The internet was still running, and he prayed it stayed up for just a bit more, at least until he found Rita.

After zoning in on his location, Judd was even more excited.

"You are only two miles from me." Judd typed. "Here is my number if you need to call me. I'm on my way."

"I don't have a phone," was the reply.

Judd grunted then stared again at the map. He made a mental picture in case it got lost. "Be there shortly. Don't go anywhere."

"I won't. I'm scared."

Judd hurried to the stairs, he moved fast, filled with exuberance. Half way down the steps his message went off again.

"Watch out for the zombies. They may be out there."

Judd stopped.

"Holy shit. I knew it. I knew it," he said to himself and simply told Rita to stay inside.

It made sense. Everyone dropped dead, of course they would rise. Ben hadn't yet, Judd didn't see any walking corpses but that didn't mean they weren't out there. Rita was probably barricaded in her home. Judd envisioned a group banging on her door, trying to get in.

He grabbed the first thing he could find as a weapon, a hammer, then got into the rental car and followed the directions.

He made it only about a mile when mangled cars on the main road blocked him from going any further. Hammer in hand, he ran the rest of the way on foot.

He kept an eye out for any creatures, but he didn't see any. The directions took him to a house on a modest residential street. There were no cars in the driveway, no 'zombies' that he could see, and he was glad. Judd didn't want to pound on the door or scream out, just in case. He sent a message as he walked to the front door.

"I'm here," he wrote as he stood on the porch.

A few seconds later, the front door flung open and Judd was pummeled with welcoming arms that latched tight around his waist. At that moment, the zombie warning made sense, considering who it came from. Judd was so grateful he got drunk and made that stupid video, or else he never would have gone to that house. Because Rita wasn't a woman after all. Rita was a child. A young boy who trembled and held on to Judd for dear life.

Judd wrapped his arms around the child, holding him. "It's okay. It's okay. What's your name?"

"Dawson," the boy replied muffled. His face buried in Judd's gut.

"You're not alone, Dawson. I'm here," Judd said. "It's gonna be all right."

Judd didn't need to know what the child had been through, he himself bore witness to the events. However, he couldn't imagine the fear Dawson experienced. It was gut wrenching to think about the kid being alone.

They stood on the porch and Judd held him while he cried while he kept telling Dawson everything was going to be fine. Even though they both knew that was the furthest thing from the truth.

SIX – PAIRING

That firm rule of 'Don't talk to strangers' went out the window, and Dawson was sure his mother would not be mad. After all, if the guy was all that bad, his mother wouldn't have subscribed to his videos. Dawson was glad she did or else he wouldn't have seen the notification of a new video. When it popped up, Dawson knew someone out there was still alive.

Lucky for the guy, Dawson was watching videos or he would have missed it. Yes, he was glad the man found him, really glad, but Dawson sensed the man needed him, too.

Just because he was a grown up, didn't mean he wasn't scared. In fact, Dawson felt bad for him. He was stuck far from home, when Dawson himself was in his own bed. It was dark and the man was so scared, he was talking funny, his eyes were as red as Dawson's probably from crying. But he sang good and wrote a fun song. Dawson watched the video three times before leaving a comment. It made Dawson calm. He needed calm, he cried a lot the night before. So much that his eyes were puffy and his eyeballs were dry. He thought he used up all his tears. That was until the man arrived and Dawson cried again.

Dawson was a hugger, so when the man showed up at his house he just grabbed on to him. He was tall guy, not real thin like his dad, nor did he have the pillow gut. Dawson felt like he was a friend, especially after the video.

After he showed up, Dawson didn't know what was next. The guy stepped in, shut the door and Dawson was a little scared.

"You aren't gonna kill me, are you?" Dawson asked.

"Nah," the man crouched down to be at his height. "Why? You ain't planning on killing me, are you?"

"Not if I don't have to."

He smiled and rubbed Dawson's hair. "Look, I'm not real good with kids, I don't have a lot experience. You know how it goes. But I like them. I think you're pretty damn brave to be standing here in front of me after yesterday."

"It was scary."

"Yeah, it was." Judd agreed.

"I liked your song."

"Thanks, it was a last minute thing."

"What now?" Dawson asked.

"Well, we'll figure that out. Did you eat?"

"Only some string cheese."

"Not a meal. Bet you have food."

"We do. My mom likes to shop," Dawson said.

"Don't all women?"

Dawson shrugged.

"Tell you what. Lights are still on, bet the water is still warm. Looks like you're still in your school uniform. Why don't you get a change of clothes, take a shower or bath, whatever kids take these days, and I'll make us some food. Sound good?"

Dawson nodded.

"How hungry are you? Little hungry? Regular hungry, or big?"

"Very big."

"Then big breakfast it is. Go shower."

"Okay." Dawson took a few steps back, then stopped. "I'm glad you're here, Mr. Heston." Then Dawson ran to his room to get his clothes. He meant his words. There was a feeling of scared that Dawson had since school. Sometimes it was less, sometimes it was so strong his whole body shook, but whatever the level, it never went away. Until Mr. Heston showed up and Dawson didn't feel as scared anymore.

◇◇◇◇

There was a phone charger on the counter and it fit Judd's phone. He plugged it in. He needed the informational resource it was.

In fact one of the first things Judd searched on the internet was how long the internet would last. Most experts agreed only a couple hour because it would be overloaded with people posting. Since everyone was basically dead, Judd figured he'd have the internet as long as the power held up. Which, according to the websites, was about a week.

He searched lots of things, including a quick tip search on handling kids. His best reference was his father so he placed himself in his father's mindset.

Cooking was something he didn't need to search. Judd had been cooking since he was thirteen. He fried up the eggs and bacon and pulled out the frozen waffles. After setting the table nice for him and Dawson, he started snooping around the kitchen for information about his parents. He knew that subject would come up.

It would have to, unless Dawson knew the fate of his parents.

"What are you looking for?" Dawson asked when he returned.

"Honestly?" Judd asked. "Just looking for stuff about your parents."

"What kind of stuff?" Dawson sat down.

Judd poured a cup of coffee and joined him. "Do you know where they are, Dawson?"

Dawson nodded and grabbed a piece of toast. "They both were working. Probably stuck there."

The last thing Judd was going to do was give the kid a reality check. "Do you know where they work?"

"My mom teaches at a school and my dad works at a bank helping people buy houses. I was waiting here for them."

"That's always good."

"They didn't come back. You got here. You think... you think the same thing happened to them?"

Judd swallowed the lump in his throat. "I don't know. If you want, I can find their work and go look."

"And leave me?"

"It would be for the best."

Rapidly, Dawson shook his head. "I wanna go."

"Dawson, if they're … if something is wrong, it won't be good. You don't need to see it."

"I didn't need to see the lawnmower eat Mr. Westerman, but I did."

"You have a …" Judd tilted his head as he looked at Dawson. "The lawnmower ate Mr. Westerman?" He asked shocked.

"He fell under it."

Judd cringed. "Oh, man. Sorry you had to see that."

"Me, too. I saw a plane fall from the sky."

"Yeah, me, too."

"You talked on the video about how many planes were in the sky. How many are left?"

"None," Judd said. "The last one, DAL4531 dropped from the sky right before midnight."

"How did you know about that stuff?"

"I looked it up. I looked up a lot of stuff. "

"Did you look up how to survive? Like hacks on surviving."

"Hacks?" Judd asked. "Never heard a kid use that term. Yep, I did. I might have to write things down."

"You can use my mom's computer and print them out."

"Little man, that's a great idea."

"Any zombie survival stuff?" Dawson asked. "I was watching the videos about it."

"Dawson, I didn't see any zombies."

"Something caused everyone to die, right. It makes sense they'll get right back up."

"Wow, we think alike. I thought the same thing."

"Have to be ready," Dawson said. "They wouldn't make movies about it if it wasn't going to happen. What other stuff did you look up?"

"Everything."

"Did you look up what happened?" Dawson asked.

"No."

"That's not everything."

"I think everyone died before they knew what happened," Judd said.

"Maybe someone didn't, you didn't, I didn't. Maybe someone posted somewhere. You have a lot of followers, you should check."

"Yeah, yeah, I do. That's a great idea, Dawson."

"Or at least check the internet for people surviving after everyone dropped over." Dawson suggested.

"I'll do that now." Judd stood and walked for the phone.

"Breakfast is good, Mr. Heston."

"Thanks, I've been …" Judd paused. "Why are you calling me, Mr. Heston?"

"You wrote the song, said that's your name. I was calling you mister cause it's polite."

"Oh. Well, you don't need to call me Mr. Heston."

"Isn't that your name? Why would you tell the world a wrong name?"

Judd didn't have a plausible answer. He could tell the boy he was drunk and being an idiot, but he didn't. "No, I mean, just call me Judd. Everyone does."

"So I don't need to call you Mr. Heston. You said on the song to call you Mr. Heston."

"Only when it matters. For now, call me Judd."

"When does it matter?"

"Um …" Judd stumbled for an answer and blurted out. "Let me think on that one."

"Where's your guitar?"

"It's in the car. I left it there. It's not far, I just wanted to get here." He took his phone from the charger and sat back down at the table.

The boy had a point. Judd needed to search for answers. What happened, what could cause it, was it only America, or was it all over the world? Plausible explanations could be found in the news or some science article. However, to discover the scope of the event, he had to rely on witnesses. There had to be others... The world revolved around the internet. It was still up for the time being. If he himself posted, someone else may have, too. He just had to look. Judd did just that while he sat with Dawson eating their breakfast.

SEVEN – RELUCTANT

The sound of nothing and smell of coffee caused Morgan to open her eyes. At first she thought she was late for work. She probably slept through the alarm clock and the auto brew on her coffee pot had long since made its pot.

'Shit', she thought. "I can't be late again. I'll get fired."

As soon as she jumped to a sitting position, a pain like she never felt cut through her side and she gasped hard, trying to catch her breath.

Her head throbbed and her forehead burned and felt tight, as did her cheeks and nose. She reached up to her head and felt a bandage. She pulled away her fingers and stared at her hand. It was bruised and brush burned. Then she remembered, the car accident. It all came back to her. The crash, the near death experience.

She was injured, from the feel of her body, she took quite a jolt. But where was the noise of the hospital? The beeping, the occasional paging of a doctor. She checked out both arms, where was the IV?

Then she took in her surroundings. She wasn't in a bed, she was on a leather couch, a hard-brown blanket covered her. Forcing beyond the pain, she sat up more. There were chairs, a coffee table and a huge reception desk.

Something wasn't right. She remembered being rescued, pulled from the car. Why wasn't she in a hospital?

Who would do this to her? Had some sick, psycho kidnapped her?

Through the corner of her eye she spotted her purse on the coffee table. It hurt her ribs when she moved her legs, surely at least one rib was broken. The pain was horrendous.

She managed to place her feet on the floor, then while securing her ribs, she reached for her purse. It hurt to reach, she inched her rear to the edge of the couch, grasping the strap. The weight of the purse pulled at her and she cringed hard in pain.

She lifted it to the couch and reached inside, feeling around until she felt her phone.

The screen was cracked, yet she was able to wake it from sleep mode.

She looked around, no one was there that she could see. Morgan could run, make an escape, the front door with a closed blind, was ten feet away, but she couldn't move. At least not fast enough, not in her condition. She selected the call pad and dialed 911.

What would she tell them?

'Hello, I was in a car accident. I think it was a couple hours ago and I have been kidnapped. I don't know where I am.'

It sounded insane but it was the truth. She hit the 'send' button to call 911.

It rang.

It kept on ringing and finally after twenty rings a recording answered informing her to hold.

"What?" she asked, breathless and in disbelief. She ended that call and immediately called Craig. That was the first person she could think to call. His phone went directly to voice mail.

"Craig," she gushed emotionally. "It's me. I need your help. This is not a ploy. I was in an accident. Someone ..." she looked up when the front door opened.

The man was a mere shadow with the sun behind him, then he stepped inside.

"Hey, you're up," he said. "That's a good sign. I'm glad." He removed a cloth from his face, and with him was some sort of odor she could smell as he came closer. She didn't recognize it though.

Then she got a look at him and the police uniform.

He was still wearing it, but had the shirt unbuttoned, exposing a white tee shirt.

"I made coffee. Electricity is still on. Did you want a cup? Are you up for drinking it, or would you prefer water?" he asked.

Morgan didn't answer, she scooted back on the couch and brought her hand to her mouth. "What is that smell?"

"Something that can't be avoided. Let me get you coffee." He walked by her and into the back of the building.

Morgan immediately dialed the phone again, she'd go through her contacts if she had to.

"I was trying to find a boat, but that was out. Trying to find some way out of the city," he said from the back. "I think I found a clear path. We may have to switch cars every ..." he stopped talking when he returned. He handed her the coffee cup, which Morgan didn't take. "That isn't going to work." He took the phone. "No one is there."

"I'm calling for help."

"Won't work."

"Take the coffee." He set it on the table. "How are you feeling? How is your head?" he reached for her.

She jumped back. "Please. Let me go. Don't hurt me and I won't tell a soul."

He laughed at her, a soft chuckle. "Morgan, I am not ..."

"How do you know my name?"

"Your license."

"Why am I here?" Morgan asked. Her heart raced out of control. "Why am I not in a hospital or home?"

"Yesterday when ..."

"Yesterday?" Morgan asked in shock.

"Oh wow," he said softly. "Shit, I figured you knew, or remembered."

Morgan shook her head.

"Morgan, what's the last thing you remember before you crashed the car."

Morgan closed her eyes to think, it took a while. "I was fighting with my husband. I .... had an anxiety attack or something and I crashed. I crashed because I had an anxiety attack."

"Anxiety attack. Describe it," he said.

"My throat closed up. I don't know ... I couldn't breathe, that's all I remember, then the crash."

"So like me, it affected you. I just can't figure out why we pulled through."

"What are you talking about?" Morgan asked. "What does all this have to do with me being here with you, Officer...?"

"Ross. Call me Ross." He reached out his hand.

"Don't touch me." Morgan panicked.

"Morgan, I swear to almighty God I am not here to hurt you. I may be the only person right now you have. Can you walk?"

Suddenly, Morgan got an eerie feeling. "What's going on?"

"You didn't cause your crash, Morgan. I can tell you ... but I think you need to see." He still extended his hand. "Please."

Reluctantly, Morgan took it and he helped her to stand. "What hurts?" he asked.

"Everything."

"You'll have that when you get smashed by several cars." Holding on to her arm, Ross helped her to the door. "Listen." He paused before pulling open the door. "You need to hold your breath, or cover your nose, okay? It's bad and it has just started."

"What are you talking about?"

"Hold your breath," he instructed and opened the door.

She didn't. She should have.

A horrible stench pummeled her, like rotting fish in the fridge mixed with a burning scent, it made her eyes water and she covered her nose and mouth when she started to gag.

"It'll get worse."

Once she got a hold of her senses, Morgan looked around.

Every single car had crashed in one way or another, some into each other, some into buildings. There was a thick haze in the air that looked like smoke. Her eyes widened and watered. "Oh my God. Were we attacked?"

Ross shook his head. "No. It's bigger than that. Much bigger."

"What happened?"

"I don't know exactly. Still trying to figure it out. But I have a feeling, all this …" he said, moving his hand about, pointing to the death. "Is just the beginning."

EIGHT – CONNECT

The website was informative, and after downloading 'How to Survive the Apocalypse, by Frank Slagel' Judd began the task of printing up the book. Dawson grabbed him a three ring binder from his father's office, then went off to find his shoes.

Judd remembered the days of being a kid and losing his shoes, but as an adult, he never understood how that was possible.

How does a person lose their shoes in their own house?

Dawson's search gave Judd time to explore his mother's computer. It was easier to search on a desktop than his phone. But no new news had posted on social media, there hadn't been a new post in over twenty-four hours, and even his *'Call Me Mr. Heston'* video only had three views.

The search for others out there was difficult, Judd knew they had to be there. Him and Dawson weren't, and couldn't be, the only ones.

Aside from printing up that book, he was productive in other ways. A simple snoop job through his mother's desk led him to his father's business card. If the information was up to date, Bill Dawson Montgomery worked as an assistant branch manager at a bank not far from Dawson's house.

His mother Rita, Judd learned was a visual arts teacher at the local high school. She also had an email in her draft folder writing to some child psychologist about how special Dawson was. She never finished and Judd guessed he'd eventually figure out what that 'special' thing meant, since Dawson and him were now survival partners.

Judd mapped the route out to find Dawson's folks. In fact, he abandoned the car not far from the bank.

That was as far as he planned, he and Dawson hadn't talked much about what was beyond searching out his parents. He supposed they had time to talk about it later. Judd also needed time to study the survival guide.

He tried again on social media, this time trying keywords and selecting all posts. He went to the Bird site and searched chirps and tried there. Judd tackled every combination of words he could think of from 'Everyone is dead' to 'Is anyone alive'.

Nothing.

"Hey, Dawson, you find your shoes yet?" Judd called out. Not that he was in a hurry to take the child to find his parents. While there was a chance his parents lived, Judd doubted it and hoped that he could get Dawson to change his mind before he was face to face, literally, with the truth.

"Found them. Be right down." He yelled from upstairs.

"Take your time," Judd replied. He turned to check the printer, and grabbed some of the pages.

"I'm ready." Dawson announced as he entered his mother's office.

"Just getting these together."

"We're coming back, right?" Dawson asked. "I'm sure my mom just needs someone to help her get home. You said cars were all over the place."

"They are and we will. We'll come back." Judd set the papers aside. 'Dawson, are you sure this is something you want to do?"

"I need to find my mom and dad. I have to."

Judd nodded. More than anything he wanted to tell the child, 'you know it may not end well, you know chances are....' He couldn't bring himself to say it. He'd cross the bridge when he got there.

"Wouldn't you want to find your parents?" Dawson asked.

He had a point. Didn't matter if a person was eight or thirty-eight, if Judd's parents were out there, he too would need to see for himself what became of them.

"You're right," Judd said. "Okay, let's ..." he stopped and looked at the screen.

"What?" Dawson asked. "What is it?"

"Oh my God."

"What?"

The search result page of the Bird site was up, but now when Judd looked an orange banner stated, 'One new chirp'.

"Shit, someone just chirped. It matched my query."

"It matched your what?" Dawson asked.

"I put in search words, some posted something just now that matched it."

"What does it say?"

Judd moved the mouse to click on it, but stopped. "Shoot. What if it's a scheduled chirp? I do those all the time. We can't get our hopes up."

"We can't know until you look. What's it say?"

Judd clicked on it. It was timestamped one minute earlier. Posted by a user name Ray of Sunshine. It simply said, "Is anyone else alive out there?"

When they read it, both of them cheered with excitement. Judd didn't know where Ray of Sunshine was and he didn't even bother to look. He simply, without hesitation, replied 'Yes', and sat back with Dawson right at his side and waited to hear back.

NINE – ANSWERS ARE NIL

"And that's it," Ross explained. "Since I brought you in here, I spent the last twenty-four hours searching for survivors, calling out, trying to find a way out of the city. We need to get out of here. You think it smells bad now, wait until later."

"I don't know how well I'll be able to walk."

"Unfortunately, you're gonna have to. At least until after the bridge. This thing hit in the middle of the day."

"This is unreal. I'm in shock, and that …" Morgan cringed. "That came out really emotionless."

"It's hard to feel anything. I know, I'm just not wanting to think too much about it. However, I'm one of those people who can't let sleeping dogs lie. I got to figure out what's going on. Do you have family? I'm taking it you don't have children?"

"No." Morgan shook her head. "No kids. I had my husband, but he left me."

"Don't have that to worry about anymore."

"Seems very small now in light of this all. How about you?" Morgan asked. "Family?"

"A whole slew. Parents, siblings, a beautiful wife and …" Ross paused, he swallowed. "Two girls. I need to get to my house. I live about four miles from here. At Greenfield."

"Ross, why didn't you go?" she asked. "You should have gone. You could have walked."

"Yeah, I could have." He lowered his head. "I've seen what's out there. If my family is alive, then they're fine and they're staying put. But if God forbid they aren't, and I left you here, I left the one person I knew for sure was alive. I didn't know if you were well enough to leave. I couldn't let you die when you were lucky enough to be alive."

"Thank you."

"Don't thank me, yet. I'm thinking by tomorrow, you should be strong enough to start walking."

"I can try now if you want."

"No, let's give you a little more time to get better. Besides, a part of me is scared to go to my house and see." He stood up. "I know we can't wait. Fires are out of control out there. My guess is people were cooking, stoves were on, and no one was there to shut them off. This place will keep burning."

"The electricity still works. Did you check the internet?"

"Oh, yeah, been off and on it all night. I found an interesting article. Small news piece, seems contact was lost with the Marshall Islands almost a full day before everything happened here."

"What do you mean contact was lost?" Morgan asked.

"Didn't say much, just that had no response from air traffic, or phone lines. All planes were cancelled. I guess it hit everywhere before Marshall Islands could become big news."

"So do you think this hit there first?"

"It's a guess. Just a guess. If this is a natural event and not manmade, then it very easily could have followed the earth's rotation. Marshall Islands is in the first time zone. Again…" he walked over to the receptionist's desk. "I'm guessing. Everything is theory."

"Well, then give me your theory on what's happening. You said earlier it was just the beginning."

"I think it is. I want to research more before we lose everything on line. It could be anything, Morgan," Ross said. "An atmospheric blip, something from space, who knows. More or less I'm gonna call it the Swifter event."

Morgan's mouth formed an 'O' as she started to speak, but paused to catch her wording. "I'm sorry. Maybe it's the head injury. You said 'Swifter', I think the cleaning mop."

"Yeah, that's what I mean. Ever see the commercials?" Ross asked. "Pretty anal person about their house broom sweeps the floor, ding dong, here's a box with a new mop with a white cloth, gets everything you missed?"

Morgan nodded.

"Think of natural disasters, disease, war, that's fate broom sweeping. Ding dong, a box was just dropped off and Mother Nature is pulling out the Swifter. The choke and drop thing was the first swoosh."

Even though it physically hurt her, Morgan chuckled. "You know they work, but they still miss particles and push them to the sides."

"Yep. That's part of my theory, we're the pushed aside particles. However, eventually with another swoop, she'll get it all."

"If every dropping was the first swoosh, I hate to think what the next will be. I appreciate your theories, but I really hope your wrong."

"Yeah," he said. "Me too."

TEN – FLAT TIRE

Ray of Sunshine never responded, despite how quickly after his post Judd had made a comment. They waited and nothing happened, finally, Judd sent one more message stating that they'd be away for an hour or so and left his phone number.

He and Dawson ventured out, aiming for the car which was not far from the bank. The entire walk, Judd just wanted to keep an eye out for a clear route back to Dawson's street, because his road was off of Broad Avenue, a main road which was pretty blocked.

The temperature was oddly high for April, pushing what Judd thought was about eighty. Much warmer than the day before. The heat caused an incredible stench to the air. Dawson had to run back into the house not ten seconds after the first time out the door.

Judd grabbed a cloth, doused it with air freshener, put the can in his back pocket and they left again.

"Did you want to see Mr. Westerman?" Dawson asked, as they walked.

"No, I'll pass."

"It's pretty sick."

"I'll take your word for it."

"Why is it so hot?"

"I don't know," Judd replied. "Maybe because there are so many fires in town. Lots of smoke you know."

"You gonna grab your guitar?"

"I'd like to."

"Why do you think that Ray guy didn't get back to us? You think he's dead?"

"I don't know."

"I had a dream everyone dropped dead."

Judd stopped walking. "That's a pretty intense dream for an eight year old. Bet you were scared."

"Not as scared as I was when it happened. I kept thinking it was a dream, a joke, the kids were pranking me. They weren't. Why is the sky so weird?"

"What?" Judd's head spun. "What are you talking about?"

"The sky looks weird."

"It's probably the smoke."

"Doesn't look like smoke."

"It's smoke," Judd looked up quickly, took a step, stopped and looked up again. Dawson was right. The sky was so bright, the clouds were orange and the blue portion looked almost pink behind them. Judd's eyes burned after only a few seconds of peering up. "Okay, I don't know what's causing it, just don't look anymore."

"Why?"

Judd grew tired of replying with, "I don't know." so he shrugged.

They made it to where they left the car. Again, Judd looked around seeing how he could move the car closer to Dawson's house, he believed he could get it nearer by taking a side street.

The car was so hot inside it was suffocating. Judd wound down all the windows, plugged the phone into the charger and pulled up the address of Rita's work.

The bank, however was only a few blocks away and they made it there in a few seconds.

Outside, Dawson sat in the car and stared at the First National Bank.

"Do you know if this is the place your dad works?"

Dawson nodded, opened the car door and stepped out.

Judd looked at his face, he looked so brave, heaving in a deep breath into his small body.

"You okay?" Judd asked.

"I think ... I think we don't need to go in there," Dawson said. "Look around. He's gonna be like everyone else. If he wasn't, he would have been home."

Judd placed his hand on Dawson's shoulder and gave a firm squeeze. "I'm going to go in and check, okay? Just so we know. You all right with staying out here?"

Dawson nodded and Judd went into the branch.

He preferred to wait outside, Dawson was sure of his father's fate. Not far from the big glass window, Dawson stood staring at the bank. His eyes teetered between focusing on seeing inside and looking at his own reflection.

It was weird. He could see himself and all the crashed cars around him. Just as focused on trying to see Judd, he saw something move behind him.

Dawson gasped in shock and spun around. Nothing was there. His heart started to beat and he faced the window again, only to hear something drop.

It caused him to jump and Dawson screamed out. "Judd! Judd!"

He wasn't going to wait and ran straight to the door, grabbing for it at the same time Judd stepped out.

"What's wrong?" Judd asked.

"I heard and saw something." Dawson grabbed on to him.

"Where? What did you see?"

"Something. I don't know. I was looking at the window. It was back there." Dawson pointed across the street.

"I don't see anything. Maybe you saw a bit of me inside."

"Maybe."

Pause.

Dawson looked up to Judd. "Did you see him? Did you find my dad?"

Judd bit his bottom lip and placed his hand on Dawson's head. "Yeah, buddy, I did. I'm sorry."

Dawson nodded, sadly. "I thought so. Let's go." He wasn't giving up hope. There was still his mother. He walked to the car, but not without looking back one more time to see if anything, or anyone was there.

The lady's voice on the phone gave them directions that took them close to his mother's school. They left the car about a block away and walked the rest of the way there.

"This is it. This is the school," Dawson said. "I've been here with my mom. I know her class. She brought me here on take your kid to work day."

"That's pretty cool. Your mom seems like a nice lady. I mean she does like my videos."

Dawson was optimistic. In his mind he kept thinking his mother just stayed to protect the kids, she didn't want to leave them alone. Judd had to break the glass on the front doors, they were locked. Dawson took that as a sign they were protecting themselves from the undead. He didn't once let it enter his mind that she wasn't fine and sitting in her classroom.

Not once.

Until they walked through the main doors, caught the overwhelming rotten smell and saw the teenage girl hanging by a belt from the railing of the upper stairwell.

She had clearly taken her own life.

Before he could react, Judd grabbed onto him, trying to shield him, but something inside of Dawson fought it. He broke free of Judd's hold and ran.

"Mom!" he called out as he raced up the stairs. "Mom!" his mother's classroom was on the second floor and Dawson didn't stop.

"Dawson! Wait," Judd yelled.

Dawson didn't. He got to the second floor, ran down the hall to the last room on the left. "Mom!"

His shoes squeaked on the linoleum as he came to an abrupt halt.

There were no students in the room. He caught his breath, felt a little better, believed the room to be empty until he saw his mother laying in the back of the room.

"Dawson." Judd said out of breath.

"Mom?" Dawson ran to her and slid to the floor. His mother was on her side. "Mom?" He shook her. "Mom, wake up." He knew by looking at her that she was dead, but he couldn't accept it. Maybe she was in some deep sleep.

Judd reached for him. 'Dawson, I'm sorry."

Dawson swiped away his hand. "Mom? Mommy? Mom!"

Judd sat down next to him. "Come on, Buddy."

It started with a simple rebellious, "No." Then he repeated it over and over, louder each time until every emotion raged out of control and Dawson screamed continuously.

He didn't want it to be happening. He didn't want it to be true. But it was.

His mother was gone and there was nothing he could do about it.

◇◇◇◇

Judd was at a loss. There was absolutely nothing he could do for Dawson, except let him go. It was painful to watch and brought back memories of when Judd found his own mother when she died of an aneurism.

He stayed on the floor with Dawson, until the boy said he was ready.

"We can't leave her like that," Dawson said. "We can't."

"Do you want me to bury her?" Judd asked. "I can get a shovel…"

"No. Can you move her from the floor. Maybe put her at her desk."

"Sure. I can do that." Judd had Dawson step aside and he lifted Rita. She had already been decomposing and her body was swollen and heavy. He carried her to the front of the room and placed her in her chair.

Dawson walked up to her and whispered. "Bye, Mom." He leaned forward and kissed her cheek. "She's so cold."

"I can bury her, Dawson."

Dawson shook his head and ran out of the room. In fact he kept on running. Judd listened to his feet as they pounded the floor, fast and furious.

He waited outside for Judd.

"I'm not going to ask if you're all right," Judd said. "I know you're not. Let's go." He placed his hand on Dawson's back.

"When we get back I think I'm just gonna go to my room, if that's okay?"

"Sure, Buddy, that's fine."

They didn't speak on the walk to the car, and Dawson stayed quiet with his head against the car door as they drove. He said only one sentence, "Don't forget your guitar."

Judd managed to get closer to Dawson's road than he did the previous day. On the other side of Broad Avenue and one street down, Judd parked the car, stuck his phone in his pocket, grabbed his guitar, strapped it to his back and walked slowly with Dawson.

As they approached the end of the street, just near Broad, Dawson's head lifted, then Judd saw. A man stood there on the corner.

With a smile, Judd looked at Dawson. "Another survivor." He tugged his arm and both of them, excitedly ran toward the man facing the other side of the street, as if waiting to cross.

"Hey!" Judd called out. "Hey!"

A few feet from him, the man turned around. He was a bigger guy, heavy, his face was sweaty and red from the heat. His thinning hair was a mess and he wore a dirty and dampened mechanic's uniform from a tire shop, the name 'Chuck' was embroidered on his chest.

"Oh, man," Judd said. "Are we glad to see you. We thought we were the only ones alive."

The man just stared at him, he didn't respond. Judd thought at first, he was in shock.

"Judd…" Judd extended his hand. "This is …" he withdrew his hand.

The man had a flat expression, staring at Judd, not blinking, not saying a word, showing no emotions, or even comprehension. There was something about him that sent a chill through Judd. Maybe he was in shock, but Judd wasn't waiting around.

He swept Dawson into his arms. "Let's go." And, after side stepping, Judd kept an eye on Tire Man, as he crossed the street with Dawson and picked up the pace.

Tire Man slowly rotated his body and watched them.

"Where we going?" Dawson asked. "What about that man?"

Judd didn't answer, he just kept going.

"Wait. You missed my street. Where are we going?"

Judd only told Dawson to be quiet until he made it far enough away. Then he cut through the back yards of houses to get to Dawson's street. He didn't want Tire Man to follow.

"Why did we leave him?"

"Shh." Judd set him down and whispered.

"Why'd we leave him? He was like us."

"No." Judd shook his head. "Didn't you notice? Something was wrong with him."

"Maybe he was scared. Maybe he was hurt."

"Maybe." Judd kept moving toward the house, but he never stopped looking behind them.

No sooner did they step into the house, Dawson slipped back into his sad state. The rush of seeing Tire Man then running from him, had faded and Dawson grabbed the family pictures and went to his room.

Dawson may have forgotten about Tire Man quickly, but Judd didn't. In fact, Judd had what he thought was an irrational reaction. He locked every door and window in the house, pulled the blinds, and cranked up the air conditioning. He checked on Dawson frequently and made him something to eat. He could hear the boy crying, but every time Judd knocked, Dawson pretended he was alright. Before eight PM, Dawson had fallen asleep.

Judd wasn't tired. He nursed a beer and sat in front of the computer staring at Ray of Sunshine's Bird account.

He wondered about the man who made the chirp, but his mind was never far from Tire Man. Who was he? What was wrong with him? Maybe the man was so shocked by the events that he didn't know how to react, or what if he were deaf and Judd just ran from him?

He rocked back and forth, staring at the screen, most of the lights in the house were out. It was quiet for the longest time, until the wind started picking up outside causing a steady rattling on the window next to the desk.

It was hypnotic, and Judd was obsessed with refreshing the Bird site.

"Reply, chirp, something." Judd stared.

Buzz. Ring.

Judd jumped a foot in the air, tipping back the chair and nearly toppling his beer when his phone rang and spun from the vibration on the desk.

With a sweep of his hand, Judd snatched up the phone, not even looking at the number. He answered the phone, just as a loud 'crack' of thunder caused him to jolt again.

"Hello."

"Judd?" the male voice asked.

"Oh my God. Yes, is this Ray of Sunshine?"

"Don't feel much like sunshine at this moment, you?"

Judd sat down. Unless Ray was visiting from abroad, his clear Australian accent told Judd he wasn't anywhere close.

"No." Judd rubbed his eyes. "No sunshine here. Where are you?"

"Osborne Park, Perth? You? Obviously American."

"Ohio." Judd exhaled, calming his nerves. Lightning flashed, four times, and a few seconds later, the thunder blasted. "I can't tell you how glad I am someone else is alive. Are you alone?"

"Not anymore. I found a few. You?"

"Just me and a little boy."

"Bet it was bad there, when it happened. Middle of the day."

"Yeah, it was, people fell off of buildings and cars crashed, I don't know how many people died that way."

"We were lucky, it happened here at 10:37 at night. We weren't the first though. Did you hear?"

"Man, I haven't heard anything. I can't find out anything."

"A shift started east of here. New Zealand, Marshall Islands, good day before it hit here. We were told about it."

"A shift? What do you mean?"

Judd pulled the phone away from his ear, when the storm grew louder outside, causing a hiss of static.

"Hello?" Judd called out. "Ray?"

"Here. Connection is getting bad. I'll try to stay in touch. Have you got the storms there yet, Mate?"

Judd glanced toward the window. "Yeah. How did you know?"

"They're everywhere," Ray said, the sound of his voice dancing in and out of static. "They're bad. Stay clear of the windows. Check the satellite feeds. Keep on top."

"Listen …"

"I have to go. Have to get secure now. Watch out for the …" A rush of line noise and the call went dead.

"What out for the what?" Judd asked. "Ray? Ray?"

Nothing.

Judd looked at the phone, the call had dropped. At least he had Ray's number to try and reach him again. He set down the phone and moved his chair closer to the computer. He didn't have any idea what Ray meant about checking the satellite feeds, and he deduced the warning was about storms.

He opened the internet, pulled up a search bar and searched for live satellite feeds.

Surprisingly, the government had a live satellite map. He learned something new.

When the image appeared, Judd didn't know what he was looking at. In fact, he thought something was wrong, because the image looked like one big swipe mark of purple and red.

It flickered, then went black.

"Swell."

The room lit up with the flash of lightening again, and suddenly it sounded like someone was running a garden hose against the window.

"You aren't shitting me, the storm is bad." Judd stood and parted the blind. He couldn't see anything because of the bush that blocked the window. He finished off the beer and went to the kitchen for another. While there, he checked the kitchen drawers and found a flashlight on the counter. The storm was loud and picked up in severity. The last time he heard wind like that, the stage was swept away. With that thought, he set down his beer and flashlight on top of the railing post and went upstairs to Dawson's room.

"Hey," he called out softly. "You awake?"

Dawson didn't answer.

He walked to the bed and listened for the sounds of his breathing, then blanket and all, he lifted Dawson and carried him downstairs just to be safe.

He placed the boy on the couch, then walked over to retrieve his beer. The second the beer touched his lips, the lights went out.

Judd turned on the flashlight. It didn't give off that much light, but then again, Judd didn't need it. The lightning was intense and the sound of water against the windows went from a garden hose to buckets.

"This is insane," Judd said. "How bad is this storm?"

Even though Ray warned him Judd walked over to the big living room window. He had to see what was going on out there.

He separated the blinds wide enough to peek out. As soon as he did, lightning flashed four times, long and strong. It not only brightened the entire street like daylight, but it illuminated the frightening sight of Tire Man standing in the torrential downpour in the front yard, not moving and staring straight at Judd.

ELEVEN – TROMP

There was no healing time, none at all, and Morgan's pain was worse. She was fine during the night when she shifted and moved in the computer chair, but once she was still for that brief sleep period, the pain was atrocious. Her head was better, every other appendage as well. It was her ribs. It looked like two of them on the right side were broken or cracked. Each breath hurt. She would have never imagined the pain.

She balked at all of Ross' suggestions, she'd ride it out with ibuprofen and follow the advice she got on line. Everything he suggested, with the exception of deep breathing practice, was old world and proven by medical experts to be incorrect methods of treating broken ribs.

When they had to move and do so quickly, she relinquished the fight and raised her arms, as best as she could ... literally.

Ross had been there, he himself broke a rib when he was younger playing baseball. He knew the pain and the treatment. He also knew what worked, and he told her so.

He had told her he suspected right away her ribs were broken and with that, had the foresight when he got supplies, he picked up bandages, pain pills and antibiotics.

Morgan hadn't taken anything more than an ibuprofen.

"I don't want to get pneumonia," she told him. "Binding causes that."

"It won't if you deep breathe and take the antibiotics. I'm not a doctor, but I know what works and what will make you feel better."

After he wrapped them Morgan realized he was right. They did feel better bound and stabilized, plus it didn't take long for that pill to kick in. It didn't make her drowsy either, it took away her fear of going outside.

Of that, she was terrified.

She spent most of the evening and night on the computer while Ross slept. She looked up everything and anything that she could think of related to what occurred. In fact, Morgan was certain she had figured it out. Or at least she was in the ball park.

Her job before everyone dropped was a risk analysist. Ever since she was a child, she planned and thought everything through, to the point it was unnerving to people.

She was always that person that said, "If we do this, then this and that could happen."

Spontaneity wasn't in her vocabulary ... ever.

She even planned their best route to get to Greenfield if they had to walk, and where they could possibly get a car and which back streets they could take that might not be blocked by crashed cars.

She wrote everything down, in case her phone died, and would have furthered her research had the power not gone out with the storm.

She had expected the storm, although not as severe, and unfortunately more was going to happen. Ross was right on that, just his reasoning why was skewed. She planned to talk to him about it, after they made it to Greenfield. She figured he needed to be in the right frame of mind for his family search.

All that went out the window when he woke her up with urgency. "We need to move. We need to move now."

She looked at her watch, it was barely daylight.

It hurt to lift her arm. "What's going on?"

"As soon as it's light enough to safely walk, we have to go. Hopefully, it'll hold. Let's get you ready."

She didn't know what ready meant, and she shook her head when he pulled out the bandage to bind her, then she felt the pain.

"I can't have *that*," Ross said. "You have to be strong and you're gonna have to move fast, this is the best way."

The pain was unbearable to even sit, but she'd managed.

"Stand up."

"What is going on?" Morgan asked as she staggered to a stand. When she did, her feet squished on the damp carpet and she lifted her head.

Ross stepped aside, walked to the door and lifted the blind.

"Oh my God." Morgan nearly fell backwards.

They were so close to the river, that had to be the reason. The storm was worse than she imagined. Water had come up to the door at least three feet. The seal was holding it, allowing only a bit of water to seep through, but a crack was forming on the glass.

"I went to the top floor," Ross said. "It looks about this deep for a while. I couldn't see too far. The back is the only way out. This gives us the street."

"How in the hell are we going to do this."

"Carefully," Ross replied.

That was when he wrapped her.

They didn't have much as far as belongings, just her purse. She placed her pills and notes in a plastic garbage bag and shoved it in her purse. In the employee break room there was a drawer full of those plastic grocery store bags. Using tape, they both wrapped their feet in them.

"I figured the water is at least three feet deep. When I open this door, that pressure is going to be bad," Ross explained. "you're not in any shape to fight that current."

"Okay .... So what choice do I have?"

Ross pointed to the receptionist desk. "You'll get up there, hold tight to the ledge, Just in case."

The desk had a lip that was a foot or so above the surface. It was a difficult climb and her feet slid from the plastic. Ross aided her up there and sat on top, holding the ledge. He walked to the door.

"Ready?" he asked.

Morgan nodded.

He appeared to be bracing his footing. One hand on the door handle, the other reached for the deadbolt. The moment he turned the lock, the need to open the door was lost and Ross wasn't ready. The pressure of the water blasted the door open, sending him flying back. He bounced off the desk and the current rushed under his feet, sweeping him across the reception area into a wall.

"Ross!"

He managed to grab the archway and hold on. His legs moved with the water as his fingers barely gripped.

Morgan felt helpless. Bodies sailed in with the water at a high speed. One hit into Ross, he lost his grip and he washed away with the water.

"Ross!" Morgan screamed.

Within a minute, the water calmed when it reached the height of the water outside.

"Ross!" she screamed again. After she lowered to her hands and knee, Morgan began to climb down. Her first thought was to find him and hope he hadn't drown.

"I'm okay!" he yelled in the distance. "I'll be right there."

She lowered her head in gratefulness. She listened to the splashing of the water and knew that was Ross making his way to her.

"Are you all right?" She asked when she saw him.

"Yeah, knocked the wind out of me." He coughed. "You ready to do this?"

Morgan nodded and Ross helped her from the desk. The water felt strange, almost slimy. Morgan adjusted the strap to her bag to lift it higher. The water came to her mid-thigh and it was hard to walk. Once outside, it was water as far as she could see. It appeared as if a city was in a shallow lake.

Bodies floated everywhere. Most of them face down. It was like walking through a pond filled with lily pads, only the green leaves of nature were replaced with earth's most precious commodity ... people. Morgan tried not to look, it wasn't their bodies that disturbed her, it was the fact they lost their lives. People like her, who went to work, had families, loved ... now everything about them, every memory they held was gone.

She couldn't move without bumping into one, despite Ross leading the way, moving them aside.

Even though he announced when she needed to watch her footing. Bodies were still trapped in cars, and she grew squeamish when she would nudge against a limb. Pushing through the water was slow and trudging. The pace would be a hindrance, but they had to keep going. The smell was a stew of many rotten things. The water wasn't cold, and the weather was still stifling hot. There was a heavy overcast to the day filled with dark gray clouds that looked violent. It was humid, very humid and sticky. They had to keep moving. They needed to get deeper into the city and away from the river, at the very least get to a higher ground or overpass. It wouldn't be long before another storm arrived.

TWELVE - STUDY

The last thing Dawson recalled was holding on to his family picture, clutching it tight to his chest while watching the video of his family at Cedar Point the year before. He watched that video over and over. He heard his mother's voice and he needed that. It was hard for him to believe that he would never see them again. They were gone.

He fell asleep covered by his favorite gray blanket, his iPad by his head propped on his pillow. When he woke up, he was still covered, still holding that picture, and sweaty, only he was on the couch. He had been dreaming about fishing with some man he didn't know, and when he woke up calling out, "Branson!" he tumbled to the floor.

It wasn't bright in the living room, and he wondered if he slept the day away.

"You all right?" Judd stepped into the living room.

"Yes. Why am I down here?" Dawson asked.

"Bad storm last night, I just didn't want you upstairs, in case the house got struck by lightning or something. I can't believe you slept through it."

"Why is it so dark?" Dawson asked.

"The power went out."

"Will it come back on?"

"I doubt it, Bud. It takes someone to flip the switch. I don't think anyone is going to do that. Are you hungry?" he asked. "You didn't eat last night."

"A little."

"Come to the kitchen. We need to also talk about what we're going to do."

Judd walked away. Dawson didn't know what he was talking about. He looked at the picture still clutched in his arms, placed it on the coffee table and went to the kitchen.

He could feel the fresh air breeze when he stepped inside. It wasn't that cool though. But it was air that had a smell to it.

"It stinks." Dawson covered his nose.

"You kind of get used to it."

Judd sat at the kitchen table, there was a ton of food spread out. Most from the fridge and freezer.

"What's going on?"

"Gonna have to cook this all up today. This is what we're gonna eat. The other stuff, the cans, boxes, that can wait. This is stuff that didn't go bad."

"How you going to cook it if there's no electricity?" Dawson sat at the table.

"I can get the stove working with a match."

Dawson lifted the flat box of pizza bagels. "How you gonna make these?"

Judd took the box. "I'll figure it out."

"Hey, Judd, you said we have to talk about what we're gonna do. What did you mean?"

"It means." Judd stopped sorting out food and folded his hands on the table. "We need to figure out our next move. We can't stay here."

"Why not?"

"Power is out. It's only gonna get hotter. We're in for some crazy weather and it looks like it's not gonna stop for a spell."

"So why we leaving in bad weather?"

"We'll wait. Tomorrow, later today. Hopefully it breaks enough. I wanna take the car far enough to get another. But we need to leave. We need water. We have enough bottle water …"

"We can go to the store. There's one right up the street."

Judd shook his head. "That's immediate, pal. We need to think long term survival. Chapter two of that book, water, food and shelter."

"We have them all. Isn't this food." Dawson pointed to the array on the table.

Judd smiled at him. "We have to look beyond all this. You and I ... we're alive. We need to stay that way. Do you have any family other than your mom and dad?"

"I have an aunt somewhere. Not around here. You want to take me there?"

"No, I thought maybe that could be a goal. We need a goal. Something to follow, to focus on. That way we can look for a place on the way. I'm thinking where we can live off the land."

"Isn't there enough food out there? People have food in their houses, we can take that."

Judd inhaled and stared. "I suppose we can." He stood up. "You want the pizza bagels?"

"Whatever you want to make."

"How about the frozen pancakes, they're almost thawed anyhow." Judd lifted them and walked to the stove. He grabbed a pan.

"I don't want to leave, Judd. I don't want to leave my house."

"I know. I really do and we can pack a bag of stuff you want to take. I think your mom and dad would want you to go where it's safe."

"How do you know this isn't safe?" Dawson asked.

Judd put the pan on the stove and turned around. "I don't. But Ray of Sunshine said…"

"You talked to Ray?"

"He called last night. I been trying all day to call him, but I want to conserve my phone. Can't charge it until I get in my car."

"What did he say?"

"We were gonna get bad storms, to look up the satellite maps. I did. The whole county is covered with this thick cloud and they weren't moving. Earth looked like it was covered in cotton candy. Last thing he said was he had to get to safety or something."

"What did that mean?"

"I don't know. We lost connection and that storm last night was bad. Trees fell down and there's about six inches of water on the street. If it rains any worse the water might get too high to drive. Chapter four, flooding, he said not to drive if the water is moving. It seems to be moving. I think it's moving, but am not totally sure."

Dawson jumped from the table.

"Whoa, hey, wait, where are you going?" Judd grabbed his arm.

"I wanna see."

"You don't need to see."

"Sure I do." Dawson pulled away.

"Dawson, don't ..."

Before he could finish, a slight rumble vibrated the kitchen. It lasted about twenty seconds.

"What was that?" Dawson asked.

"I don't know." Judd answered softly.

"Maybe it's a rescue truck."

"It's not a rescue truck."

"I'm gonna go see. I also want to see the flood."

"Dawson," Judd said strong. "You don't need to ..."

Dawson didn't listen. Judd said the street had water, and a tree fell down. He had never seen anything like that. He ran to the living room and pulled on the door. It was locked. After undoing the bolt, he grabbed the handle and pulled.

"Dawson, don't open that door."

Too late. Dawson opened it. He was rendered breathless for a moment and near ready to scream.

Judd slammed the door and locked it, placing his body against it.

"Judd, why is that mechanic man standing in the yard?"

"I don't know. That's why I didn't want you to open the door. I didn't want you to get scared."

"Are you?"

"Heck yeah," Judd said.

"How long has he been out there?" Dawson asked.

"All night."

"All night!"

Judd facially cringed. "I know. I know. I'll handle him." He walked over and peeked out the blind. "Just got to figure out how and why."

THIRTEEN – BOURBON, TEARS AND GUESTS

Having lived in the Pittsburgh area most of her life, Morgan had never been to Greenfield. She heard of it, and for some reason she attached a bad rap section of town to it. She supposed it was like any other area, it had its shares of trouble, but there was a certain charm to the suburb. She just wished she was seeing it under better circumstances.

From where they were in downtown Pittsburgh, it was nearly five miles to Greenfield. She had set a route that was dismissed pretty quickly by Ross. Seeing how he was a police officer, she left it to his expertise. His route added a mile or so. Morgan didn't fret it, she walked further when she had gone to Vegas.

She believed at first they were looking for a car. It didn't matter, though. It was Pittsburgh, there were very little stretches of road where cars didn't block the way, at least a normal size car wouldn't get through.

The water remained high well out of downtown, beyond Duquesne University. It eventually stayed steady at ankle length, occasionally turning into a damp surface. Pittsburgh was a city of hills and slopes, if by chance the town was submerged in water, than they were in trouble.

They walked a main road that was blocked by overturned buses and cars, it was a mess.

The streets were empty and devoid of life. They passed the main hospital, and smoke rose from the roof. Fire had ravaged the entire building.

Every step she took, every painful step, Morgan hoped to see someone.

She didn't.

Sadly, seeing bodies was fast becoming common place.

They didn't speak much and they didn't discuss what was next after Ross' house. Morgan actually had nowhere to go, no one she wanted to look for. She supposed she could look for Craig, but they had been together long enough she felt his fate.

He was gone.

She realized as they walked she didn't know Ross. Only that he had a wife, kids, a big family and was a cop. Other than that, he was a mystery. He didn't ask any questions of her other than was she hurt and did she have kids.

He was a stranger to her and she had no choice but to place her trust in him. Either that or go off on her own which didn't make sense.

A little over half way on their journey, Ross veered off toward a squad car. The vehicle had crashed into a bus stop, the front end was like an accordion.

"Are you wanting to take the car?" she asked.

"No." Ross opened the door. "Ah, man."

"Do you know him?" Morgan asked of the dead police man slumped over toward the passenger seat.

"Yeah, yeah, I did." Ross reached inside and grabbed the radio microphone. He depressed the button. Nothing. He reached inside again and tried the ignition. "It's still in the on position. It ran out of gas."

"Like a lot of cars. It goes to figure," Morgan said. "They crashed and never shut off the car, they ran out of gas and the battery died. "

"That makes sense. Ross replied.

I have a radio at home. We'll try that." He moved away.

She wanted to ask, "Radio who?" She didn't. Morgan walked slowly, never once did Ross complain about her speed, or to tell her to "Keep up." He kept it steady, and Morgan did her best to stay close. When she drifted too far behind, he'd stop, wait, then move again.

Once they neared Greenfield, they hit the flooded area again, with water rising to her knees. A light drizzle started to fall. Morgan held out her hand and looked to the sky. A faint sound of thunder rumbled in the distance.

Ross' house was on a hill and had a safe and dry road. The river had spilled over at the bottom of his street forming a large pond. His home was near the top of the street. He paused as he stood on the sidewalk before the small front yard staring at the two story, gray siding home.

"You alright?" Morgan asked.

"Just getting up the courage before I go in."

"I understand."

"This is going to go two ways. I'm going to go in there and my family will be fine, or they won't. If they're fine, we all figure out the next step. If they're not, you and I need a direction because I won't want to stay here. I just can't. "

She hated sounding like a broken record, but "I understand," was the best response she could come up with.

Ross' house had a great huge front porch. There was no furniture on it, they probably hadn't put it out yet. She took a seat on the steps, catching her breath, wiping the sweat from her brow. She'd wait there while Ross went inside his house. It was his to face and his to face alone.

<><><><>

There were three things that could be found in nearly every Pittsburgher's home. Chipped Ham, Heinz Ketchup and something Steeler related. Ross had those and he also had something else … a bottle of bourbon. He never ran dry, there was never less than half a bottle. That was just his thing.

He swore he could have drank the entire bottle when he saw the body of his three year old daughter on the living room floor. At first he thought she was alive, that somehow she survived. Her back was facing him, her blanket over her and she lay on her pillow in front of the television. She wasn't.

That's where she was and what she was doing when it happened.

His wife was at the kitchen table and his five year old daughter was still in bed.

A part of him knew and he felt they wouldn't be alive, but he was hopeful, and prayed a lot during the walk there.

Once he found them, he cried. Silently and into his fist, biting his hand trying to take away the pain of his loss. It would never go away, like his badge, he'd wear it on his soul forever.

There would be plenty of time to cry and grieve, but it was hard being in the house. He grabbed the bourbon, took a big drink, sought out the radio from the basement, grabbed his wife's car keys from the table in the living room and went to the front porch.

"I have a battery for this in the house. I'm gonna pack somethings and then we'll leave." He set down the radio and handed Morgan the keys. "Can you put this in the car? It's that blue smart car up there." He pointed two doors up.

"Oh, Ross, I am so sorry."

Ross nodded. "You're about my wife's size, I'll grab you some clothes. You need fresh clothes, too."

"Thank you."

Ross went back inside. He drank some more bourbon, grabbed a duffle bag and packed some clothes. Not much, he could get more on their journeys, wherever that would be. He grabbed food, water, and his extra gun. Before he did all that, he carried his youngest daughter and placed her in bed. He did the same for his wife and covered his family.

After he finished packing, he sat on the bed. He had been in the house a while, probably longer than he should have. He needed it. But it was a curse. The longer he stayed in his house, the more he thought about his purpose.

What purpose did he have? His wife was gone, his children, more than likely the rest of his family. He thought about his revolver and if he really wanted to make a journey, or was he already at the end of his journey?

In a moment of weakness he racked the chamber and lifted the weapon near his chin.

It was possible he would have pulled the trigger, he would never know.

Morgan called his name. "Ross."

The entire time he was in that house she never called out to him, bothered him or came inside. She gave him his time. So why call him now? She said his name once and there was something about the way she said it.

He stood from the bed, grabbed the two bags and headed down the stairs.

"Ross, you need to come out here."

He shouldered the bags and pushed open the screen porch door. He barely stepped out, about to ask her what was wrong, when he saw.

About a dozen people stood in the street.

They just stood there watching, arms at their sides all spaced apart a foot or so from each other.

"Something is wrong with them." Morgan looked over her shoulder, standing at the top step.

At first, Ross entertained the ridiculous notion that they were dead and had risen. They looked very much alive. "You got the keys?" Ross asked.

"Yes."

"Let's get to the car."

"Where are we going?"

"Just move," Ross instructed. He had his revolver still in hand and they walked down the steps. When he reached his yard, Ross recognized one. Tanner Stewart. Tanner lived a block over and his daughter was in preschool with Ross' five year old. He also knew him from being on the force, he had arrested Tanner twice for bar fighting.

But that was only one. He knew everyone on their street, so why did he only know one person. Who were the others?

They were dirty and sweaty, but they looked almost hypnotized.

"Why are they staring?" Morgan asked.

"I don't know. Did you try talking to them?"

"Look at them. Would you?"

Ross ushered her quickly to the car, when they arrived the group of people all turned and faced them. He tossed the bags in the car. "Get in." he instructed, then opened the driver's door and reached in with the keys, starting the car. "Get in!"

Morgan walked around to the passenger's side, continuously looking back at the group. She opened the door.

Ross took a step away from the car.

"What are you doing?" she asked.

"Get in. I'll be back."

"Ross!"

He took a few steps back toward the group of people, looking over his shoulder once to make sure Morgan was inside the car, then he walked directly to Tanner.

Tanner stared outward, not even looking at Ross.

"Tanner." Ross called his name. "Tanner." He snapped his finger in his face.

Tanner's eyes shifted and locked with Ross.

"Tanner, are you okay? Can you hear me? Can I help you with …?"

Before Ross could finish, Tanner expression unchanged, snapped out his arm and he gripped on to Ross' mouth. His thumb pressed against one cheek, while his fingers dug into the other. He squeezed so tight, Ross swore his teeth were going to pop out of their sockets.

He couldn't even say a word, his hand was cutting off his air. He reached up, trying to pull the hand away. He saw the rest of the group approaching.

Ross was a big guy, strong too, and he couldn't free himself.

In a final attempt to pull away, Ross struggled out the word, "Stop. Please." Then lifted his revolver, placed it to Tanner's chest and fired.

The grip didn't release and Ross fired two more times until he was finally free.

Tanner dropped to the ground and Ross fumbled to find his footing while aiming outward. He expected the others to immediately come for him, but they didn't. Lowering his weapon, Ross turned and ran to the car.

He didn't say anything to Morgan. He slammed the car door, put it in gear, and looked once more in the rearview mirror, before he sped off.

FOURTEEN – DAZED

"My phone is one bar," Ray said. *"Sorry, I can't talk anymore. I'm buried in eight feet of water, and we're trying to get out. It's getting higher. Storms haven't stopped."*

"Have you had any earthquakes?" Judd asked.

"Some. Minor. Nothing compared to the water. It's the storms. That much water dumping in the ocean can shift plates. Don't they teach you that in school?"

"Oceans, I'm in Ohio. There are no oceans close. There's a lake."

"I have to go."

"Wait!" Judd yelled. *"One more question. Have you seen ... have you seen any strange people just lurking around."*

Silence.

"Hello?" Judd called out.

"The quiet ones."

"That would be a good name for them."

"Yes. More and more are showing up. They didn't die, they just took a while to get up. Like they were in a coma. I think. Yeah."

"What's wrong with them?"

"I don't know. I just avoid them. They aren't good."

"So it's a virus."

"I don't know that either. I deliver pizzas for a living, I'm not a ...."

That was it. The end of the call. Probably the last he would speak to Ray of Sunshine. Judd was rattled and he wanted to take away something from the call, but he couldn't remember what all Ray had said.

"He's in a big flood," Judd told Dawson as he kept looking out the window at Tire Man.

"Did he say anything about him?" Dawson asked.

"Not much." Judd hadn't bitten his nails since he was ten, yet there he was chomping away as he looked out the window. "They aren't good. Could be a virus."

"So he's a zombie. He doesn't move fast like World War Z. He's slow."

"I don't think he's a zombie. He was sweating yesterday. He's alive. Like that movie Twenty-Eight Days later."

"They ran in that movie. Super strong, too."

"You're eight. Why were you watching that movie?"

"I was allowed."

Judd bit a nail and peeked out. "This isn't good. I have to do something."

"You wanna kill him?"

"Yes. I mean no. I mean …" Judd looked at Tire Man. He just stood there, staring back. He stood in the same spot all night. He hadn't moved, in fact, his feet were sinking in the mud. "He's scary."

"Think you can take him?"

"Probably not."

"Why don't you see what he wants," Dawson suggested.

"We tried talking to him yesterday, remember. He didn't say a word. He just … stared. He's scaring the hell out of me and I don't like being scared. There's nothing in that survival book about catatonic lunatics."

"What's catatonic?"

"Don't worry about it." Judd bit his lip. He couldn't leave him standing there, he was unpredictable and dangerous. Judd was supposed to be protecting Dawson and he was more scared than the child.

How was he going to leave with Dawson if Tire Man was there, out there waiting? "Okay that's it." Judd backed away from the window.

"What are you doing?"

"Do you have a baseball bat around here?"

"In the closet." Dawson pointed to the one next to the front door. "Are you gonna beat him with a baseball bat? Make sure you hit him in the head."

"He's not a zombie. I'm gonna scare him away. I don't want to beat him." Judd opened the closet. A wooden bat was on the floor perched against the wall. "It would probably break on him." As he clutched the bat he felt the nervousness creep up and he jumped when thunder blasted. He could hear the instantaneous downpour hit against the house. Judd looked up. "Swell."

"It's raining again."

"I know." He shut the closet door and reached for the front door. "If something happens to me. Just ... just ... good luck. I don't know what to tell you." He opened the front door. "Jesus." He took a breath of courage and stepped out.

Tire Man stared at him.

Judd jumped a little when the door slammed. Another breath and he stepped from the porch. "I can do this. I can do this. Think big. Think angry. Be intimidating." He raised the bat that raised his voice. "What do you want!" Judd blasted.

He stepped off the porch into the pouring rain. His feet melted into the soft mud and water on the lawn.

He charged toward Tire Man. "Go away!" He moved closer. Tire Man didn't change expression. "Didn't you hear me!" Judd blasted in his loudest voice. "You got three seconds to go or I swear to God I am gonna bash you. You hear me?!"

Nothing from Tire Man.

"One." Judd stepped closer, it rained so hard, the water pooled in his eyes blurring his vision. "Two." He swiped the water from his eyes and moved within three feet of him.

He had played baseball all of his life, softball when he was older. He was good, he was a slugger and Chuck the Tire Man was a threat. Something was wrong with him, and as much as Judd wasn't violent, as much as he hated to hurt anyone, he couldn't take the chance with Dawson in the house. Tire Man was a big guy and Judd knew, he had one shot. It had to be good, or else he could be in trouble.

"Three!" Full force he lifted the bat and like stepping into the plate, he moved his leg forward and with all his might brought forth the bat.

A split second before connection, inches from his target, Tire Man lifted his left hand, tilted his head and closed his eyes while making a noise. A groaning noise that sounded like a cat, as if he had no vocal chords, ability to talk or hear anything.

Judd stopped. His eyes widened.

Tire Man lifted his hand again and flinched.

"What the hell?" Judd said, and lowered the bat in shock.

FIFTEEN – DIRECTION

The blinking yellow stop light told Ross and Morgan that the town twenty-five miles north of Pittsburgh still had power. Once they made it out of the city and to the expressway, it was easy to maneuver around the cars. Rush hour was over when everyone dropped, and HOV lanes were clear and empty because they were closed at that time.

It was smooth sailing until the expressway met the interstate, then it was quite a bit of weaving. The tiny smart car worked well, but performed poorly when they ran into wet areas. For that reason alone, they needed a bigger vehicle.

Although, Morgan had no idea where they were going.

"We'll figure it out when we stop," Ross told her.

Morgan wasn't a go with the flow person, it made her antsy. She didn't bring it up to Ross because she knew he was dealing with a lot. His hands shook a lot when he drove and she really wished he'd stop sipping from the bourbon bottle as if it were a bottle of water clutched between his legs. She wanted to blame the booze for the shakes. Like Ross was some alcoholic who needed a fix, but she was with him the entire previous day and unless he was hiding his adult beverage, that wasn't the reason.

The tremors were brought on by emotions. He assumed that his family was gone and then he had the confrontation with the crazy people. It was a lot to handle.

She was happy when she saw that flashing traffic light, it signified to Morgan they were going to stop. It started to rain again, not quite as hard as the night before, but it was steady.

It was already mid-day, and without a plan, Morgan had no idea where they would stop for the night. They needed direction.

She also needed Ross to talk to her. That was something he hadn't done until they stopped the car at a convenience store and gas station named Sheetz. It was a common store to see in the area, the 'It' place for gas and decent late night food.

An SUV was parked by a pump, the nozzle wasn't connected and that meant they either pumped the gas already or were just about to.

Ross stepped out of the car. "We should be good here from any flooding. The elevation is good." He moved to the SUV and opened the driver's door. "The keys are here." He said as he started it. "Full tank, too. I think they have gas cans inside. I wanna fill some. I'll unload the car..." He rested his arm on the door. "I saw a sign for a motel up the road. We should stop there, even though it's early. You look pretty pale and should rest. How are you feeling?"

"I'm not feeling too bad. The pain pill is still working. I'd like to unwrap my ribs and redo them. Plus, you know, change into dry clothes."

"I bet. Me, too." He went back to our car and opened the back, grabbing one of the bags. He pulled out a tee shirt and a pair of those stretch and comfortable pants that fit tighter. "I didn't know what size you wore in shoes. She wears an eight." He handed her sneakers.

"They will work, thank you."

"Meet you inside."

She took the clothing and her purse and headed toward the store.

"Morgan," Ross called her. "Want me to go check it first?"

"No, I'll be fine."

"Be careful."

Morgan nodded. She probably would have thought the 'careful' was unnecessary had they not ran into the group of people outside Ross' house.

She kept her eyes peered and when she got to the store, she looked around. The air conditioning was on and it felt good, the odor wasn't as bad as it was outside either.

Once in the store, she saw the toppled ribbon that marked off the waiting line for the register, two customers were on the floor. She didn't see any employees, they probably were behind the counters.

By the soda machine was the body of a construction worker, he still wore his reflective vest. She stepped over him, grabbed a cup and filled it just a little with soda. It was cold and tasted good.

After spotting the rest room sign, she made her way there. The tiny health and beauty aids section was near there and she grabbed a comb that was ridiculously priced, a bar of soap and a roll of paper towels.

An employee mopping the floor had dropped not far from the rest room, Morgan had to step over him.

Once in the bathroom, she double checked the stalls, then she opened the towels, laying a bunch on the floor to have a clean spot to stand on. She was a mess, her face was dirty and injured, her hair looked tangled and muddy. If she could bend over the sink to wash it she would have, but she would wait until the hotel. A shower would be best. She undressed and threw away her clothes.

Undoing the binding felt so good, almost the same free feeling of taking off her bra at the end of the day. She took deep breaths while she washed up. Paper towels and a bar of soap did a great job. She needed to clean up so her injuries didn't get infected, she had no idea what was floating in that water.

Ross hollered in to check on her, then said he was filling gas cans, he'd be back and for her to get supplies.

She acknowledged his request and continued on. She combed her hair and pulled it as best as she could into a ponytail. It hurt to raise her arms, then she did an adequate job of rewrapping her ribs.

Morgan took a while, but she felt so much better, and when she stepped out of the bathroom and looked to the right, she smiled.

She remembered when Sheetz got their state permit to sell single serving beer and malt beverages and one of those Margaritas in a can sounded good while she sought out something to eat. She was hungry.

She visually scanned the cooler, finding one of those margaritas on the shelf to the right. She opened the glass and reached in. Just as she touched the can, she gasped and stepped back, when a woman in an employee smock stood in the cooler directly behind the shelf.

She was one of them. Her eyes were dead and she stared blankly at Morgan.

For some odd reason, Morgan wasn't scared. The woman must have been in there for days, she had a blue and hypothermia look to her, her lips were white and she huffed shallow breaths.

Keeping an eye on her, Morgan quickly grabbed the can and shut the cooler. She retrieved the mop and stuck the end of it through the handles to brace the doors. She popped open the can and sipped while watching the woman in the cooler for a few seconds.

Ross was still outside and while there were a bunch of snacks in the store, Morgan needed something with substance.

Figuring since the electricity was on, chances were there were items in the fridge that were still good. It was only two days since the event happened.

The grease in the fryers was cold, and they were off. Probably an automatic shut off to prevent fires. She grabbed a clean cloth, wiped off the counters and then after pulling a pack of buns, she opened them and laid them all out. She would make some sandwiches for them both.

She pulled out the luncheon meats, sipped her margarita, then through the corner of her eyes, spotted one of those blenders for frozen coffee drinks.

"Oh, wow." she paused in the sandwich making to follow the directions on the wall and make herself a coffee shake.

It actually went well with the margarita, sipping through the straw was tough, it hurt her ribs.

She had both beverages going when she began her sandwich making stint.

"That's quite a contrast of drinks," Ross said.

Morgan wasn't expecting his voice and jolted a little. "I was thirsty."

"I see that." Ross stood on the other side of the counter.

"Then I saw these." She held up the coffee. "It's refreshing."

"You look better."

"I washed my face. The pain pill is starting to wear off. Hence this…" She held up the margarita.

"Did you grab supplies?"

"No, I'm making sandwiches right now."

"Good thinking."

"Ross," Morgan paused in her sandwich making. "You aren't going to go off on your own or kill yourself, are you?" She listened, his footsteps stopped.

"Why would you ask that?"

"A feeling. You don't talk to me. You shut down."

"There's nothing to talk about."

"I don't believe that. We're it, well with the exception of those people that are strange and the lady in the cooler."

"There's a woman in the cooler?" Ross asked.

"One of those Starers," she said. "We're it. I want to know who I'm traveling with and you should, too."

"Did you examine everything when you were married."

"I did. This situation makes me think you're planning to kill yourself. It makes sense. You lost everything. I mean, it's your choice. I will ask you not to, I hope that you wouldn't, but it's your choice. I just ask if you do, please let me know so I can be prepared and maybe get a chance to talk you out of it."

"You won't have to. I won't leave you or kill myself." he said. "I faced that … I almost did."

The bread dropped from her hand and she turned around.

"When I found my family, my gun, I just … had a moment of weakness. Then you called my name. I put the gun down."

"If you have a moment of weakness will you let me know? I'll try to help you."

"I will," he replied. "What about you? Are thinking about it?"

"Not right now," Morgan replied. "I did months ago. When my husband left me for some woman with three kids. That was fleeting, though. No, I didn't really lose anything. I didn't have friends, my family had already passed. I had no children. The way I see it, my ex-husband is dead so I don't have to think about him with another woman, I have no deadlines on my job, I don't have to worry about my high insurance payment and I'm out of debt."

Ross chuckled.

"You smiled. That's impressive considering everything."

"Well, I thought what you said was funny. I mean ..." Ross' hands went to the counter.

Morgan braced as well when the ground shook. Things clattered and the ground swayed.

"Are you kidding me?" Ross asked. "Was that an earthquake? An earthquake in Pennsylvania?"

"Probably. It's not the first. There's been many. You just don't feel them." Morgan answered almost nonchalantly, wrapping the sandwiches, placing them in a bag.

"You're not phased?"

"Not at all. I was expecting it. You've shared your theories." She handed him the bag. "When we settle for the night, I'll share mine."

"Share now."

"It's a little more difficult than that. My job was to be pretty anal," she said. "I have visual aids."

SIXTEEN – VISION

The prior evening, before the lights went out, before he heard from Ray of Sunshine, Judd read Dawson's mother's email. He was curious after finding the Dawson is 'special' email what it all meant. To him Dawson was a normal boy, not much different than Judd remembered being at that age.

An email from Dawson's teacher expressed concern about Dawson's lack of being in touch with reality. How he would easily escape to a different mental world when things weren't how he wanted them. Dawson's mother insisted that her child had an odd and keen sense about him. He often said things, or told made up stories, that somehow would happen or come true.

His teacher dismissed that. Judd guessed that was the reason she was writing the psychologist.

Dawson was unique. Sometimes he seemed to childlike, maybe even younger than eight. Other times he seemed different and reasonable. Like after Judd went for Tire Man with a baseball bat.

The second the Tire Man flinched, Judd couldn't hit him. He was afraid of Judd and couldn't communicate.

Yet, Judd wasn't completely trusting, After all, Chuck the Tire Man still stood in the yard staring with that dead pan look.

Judd simply carried the bat back into the house and locked the doors.

"Is he deaf?" Dawson asked.

"What do you mean?"

"I mean maybe that's why he didn't respond. He's deaf."

"I don't think so."

"Good thing you didn't kill him," Dawson said. "I can't believe you wanted to kill a deaf guy."

"Dawson, I don't think he's deaf. Look at him. Something is not right."

"Yeah," Dawson said. "He's standing in the middle of the yard. It's raining out and he doesn't notice or know anything."

"That's exactly it," Judd said. "Brilliant. He doesn't know anything."

"Think maybe his mind got erased?" Dawson asked. "One time my tablet fell in the toilet."

Judd looked at him oddly.

"It wouldn't start, but after my mom put it in rice, it did. However, it wasn't the same and we had to redo the whole thing. She kept saying we restored it. You think maybe he fell like everyone else, but when he woke up he was restored, so he's like a new tablet."

"Holy crap," Judd scratched his head. "That's pretty freaking brilliant dude."

"To make him the way he was you just have to download things. Teach him."

"Maybe. But I am not ... teaching him anything." Judd walked away.

"Why not? Don't you feel bad for wanting to kill him?" Dawson followed him into the kitchen.

"No, absolutely not. Hopefully by tomorrow he'll be gone. Even if he's not, we have to go."

"Go where?" Dawson asked.

"I don't know. I wouldn't even know where to begin." Judd sat at the table.

"Does the survival book say anything?"

"Just to keep moving, look for others but avoid dangerous groups," Judd said.

"That doesn't sound very helpful."

Judd shook his head. "It's not. We do need to go. The weather is bad, it's getting worse and I think we need to get away from the city. With all the bodies out there, it's not good. So ..." Judd folded his hands on the table. "Any suggestions?"

Dawson darted away into the other room and returned with a brochure. "Here. Can we go here? We were supposed to go there in three weeks. We were even getting a couple of days off school. My dad was gonna have a con... something."

"Conference?" Judd asked.

"Yeah, that's it. He was gonna do that and my mom was taking me to do the fun things. So can we?"

Judd looked down at the brochure. On the cover was a family on an amusement park ride and another picture was of a small storybook town. "Branson, Missouri. Wait ...wait ... you woke up this morning shouting Branson."

Dawson nodded. 'I was dreaming about it. I dreamt some man on a hill was waving his arm saying come to Branson."

Judd looked at Dawson then down to the pamphlet. More than likely, Dawson's dream was because he was thinking of his parents. However, just on the outside chance that Rita was right and this was one of Dawson's special moments, Judd wasn't going to dismiss it. Branson was a distance away, but it looked nice. Judd knew when they finally left, they had to have a place to aim for. The affordable and fun family vacation spot of Branson, Missouri was a path to follow. Besides, a destination and direction was far better than wondering around aimlessly hoping to find a suitable end game.

SEVENTEEN – PLAUSIBLE

Ross gave a lot of thought to what Morgan asked. Did he want to kill himself? He was glad he was honest and told her that it had crossed his mind. Even though he didn't want to die, he still had no idea why he wanted to live.

The rain was steady. Oddly heavy and steady and there didn't seem to be an end in sight. When he commented on it, Morgan kept saying, "It makes sense." Almost like a verbal trailer to her big theory.

"Morgan, this isn't a company presentation," Ross told her. "What do you think happened?"

"Wait."

He groaned about her response as they made their way, convenience store bags packed, to the Motel 6. It was difficult to figure out what rooms were empty and what rooms weren't. The last thing he needed to do was find a room with bodies.

The computer system was rocket science to him. They figured it out but ended up just staying in the lobby. It had the small table area where the hotel served continental breakfast and the lobby had two couches.

Ross cleared the three bodies from the lobby and Morgan found an empty room and used that to shower. After Ross had gotten the lobby in order he set up his radio he brought from home and then found some blankets. Then he too took a shower and changed into clean clothes.

He felt better after cleaning up and changing clothes and was surprised when he returned to the lobby and found Morgan had set one of the tables for a meal.

"That's odd," he said.

"You don't have to sit here with me. I just thought it would be nice to stop and eat. As much as you say I need to heal, you do as well."

"Thank you." He pulled out a chair and his eyes drifted to the lobby window. "I can't believe how bad it's raining. Please don't tell me it makes sense."

"It does though." Morgan said a bit frustrated he kept dismissing her idea before he heard it.

Ross sat down. "Are you gonna tell me your theory?"

"Yes." Morgan lifted her purse, reached in and then placed a stack of folded papers on the table.

"What's this?"

"Visual aids."

"You printed up things to support your theory?"

Morgan nodded.

"So why don't you just tell me?" Ross asked.

"Last night, before the lights went out, I went on line. I started thinking about what happened, people just dropping like that. I felt like I was suffocating which tells me something in the air changed. Even just a smidgeon, it could cause asphyxiation. You called it an atmospheric blip."

"Yes, I remember," Ross said.

"Anyhow I thought what if it was a chemical weapon or virus, how would it get across the globe, I started looking at prevailing winds, global winds, and jet streams." She lifted out a sheet of paper and unfolded it.

"Westerlies and trade winds I assume."

"Yes, now bear with me." Morgan said with irritation.

"Oh, I have nowhere else to go. Go on." Ross replied sarcastically.

"A weapon would dissipate becoming less deadly. How do you get everyone on earth to drop dead at the same time? I kept thinking atmosphere."

"Everyone didn't drop at the same time. I think it started in the Marshall Islands."

"Or that area, so I started searching. Atmosphere, oxygen, that sort of stuff. Then bam! I found it."

"Okay, I'm game. What?"

"Geoengineering and cloud seeding."

Ross sat back. "Geo what?"

"Geoengineering is when you deliberately manipulate the climate and weather to fight the effects of global warming."

"Weather manipulation, like the HAARP. Morgan said.

So you think this geo thing caused people to drop dead?" Ross asked shaking his head.

"It's two things. Cloud seeding being the start. It's been going on since the nineteen fifties," she said. "United States did it all the time. They fly a plane, drop chemicals into a cloud, which produces rain. That's the simple method... however..." She pulled another sheet of paper forward. "China does it on a grander scale. The night of the 2008 Olympics they launched eleven hundred rockets into the sky to prevent rain. They don't drop down on the clouds they shoot rockets up. They've been doing this for decades. Fire a thousand rockets for rain, fire a thousand rockets for dry. China really took an extreme route to manipulate their climate. I'd say look it up, but the internet is now down."

"That was fast."

"Yeah," Morgan said. "Think about it. Rockets, Ross. Every major holiday, every national day, they do this. Here's where it gets good and makes total sense. Three days ago, they launched fifteen hundred rockets in an attempt to create snow, and New Zealand, with help from the UN, on the same day did the same thing only they wanted it for drought. All you need is for them to miss the mark and punch into the mesosphere. Even as far-fetched as it sounds, what if it was just done one time too many?"

Ross took in what she said, listening intently, rubbing his face. He looked at her perplexed.

"Now you have a breach of atmosphere, the weather goes haywire, and we get crazy storms. All that water dumping into the ocean at once causes the plates to shift, and now we have earthquakes and volcanic eruptions. Things will get messy fast and worse than anything we've seen."

"So in a nut shell, rockets fired to the sky one too many times, punch a hole into the mesosphere, the oxygen balance goes off a smidgeon, people choke and die, then the weather goes haywire. Explain us and how we're alive"

"I can't explain you, but I know me, my heart was racing out of control, what if that had something to do with it. When you're anxious, you're breathing is off, it becomes faster. What were you doing?"

"Trying to stay calm."

"See?" Morgan nodded. "This is it."

"What about the, what did you call, them Starers?"

"They suffered lack of oxygen to the brain." Morgan said matter of fact. "When they woke, they were able to function just not the way they remember so they act on instinct."

Ross mumbled his thoughts. "Instinct. Tanner was violent ... no." He stood up. "No. This is science fiction. While I appreciate this theory, I really do, but please forgive me when I say this is crazy."

"It's plausible." Morgan stated emphatically.

"You did all this work, all this research, why?" Ross asked curiously.

"I need to know what happened."

"But you'll never know," Ross said. "Ever! Not for certain."

"This feels right," Morgan said quietly.

"Did you ever stop to think it was just an act of God, that maybe God said enough is enough."

Morgan laughed.

"That's funny?"

"Yeah, it is. I can't just accept and say," She deepened her voice. "Oh God did this. I can't. Besides, didn't the bible say he would never destroy the earth again?"

"No," Ross answered. "He would never flood the earth again."

"There you have it. We're probably gonna get a flood. A big one, too. All this rain, earthquakes, shifting ... flood. If that happens it's not God or else he broke His promise. This..." She tapped on the table. "Is something. If we, or at least I ... follow this theory, I can at least rationalize what is happening."

"All this ..." he sat back down and shuffled through the papers. "Why did you print a picture of the globe."

"Trade winds and Westerlies? I was trying to see if maybe there was a pattern that this atmospheric blip followed. Maybe areas that weren't hit by the oxygen depletion."

"And you think there might be some area?"

"Yeah, at least not hit as bad."

"Like where?" Ross asked.

"Um ... middle America, Kansas, Colorado and a little west."

Ross laughed.

"Oh, so now you're laughing at me?"

"The whole world dropped dead except middle America." Ross couldn't help laughing again.

"I'm not saying that as fact, I was just ..." Morgan stopped her thought.

A hiss of static rang out on the radio and Ross jumped up so fast his chair fell backwards.

"This is NP67, QST all locations. Do you copy? Anyone there?"

Ross rushed over.

Static.

"This is NP67, QST all locations, Do you copy? This NP76 QTH, Branson, Missouri."

Upon hearing the location of the radio operator, Ross looked at Morgan and she just smiled back at him, feeling vindicated.

EIGHTEEN – DIVIDE

By the next morning the tremors were frequent. They were similar to labor, each one getting longer with shorter intervals in-between. Judd was extremely worried, he didn't know what they were building to, but it was something big. By morning it was time to go.

They had packed a lot of supplies to take with them, he wrapped his guitar in a garbage bag and duct taped it. He just wished they had a car at the house because looking at a map, he believed he found a series of backroads that would get them to a highway. They had to walk to the car, and in the hard falling rain it wasn't going to be easy.

"Maybe we should just stay and wait until it stops," Dawson suggested.

"No," Judd told him. "It's not stopping and it doesn't look like it's stopping anytime soon."

"How we gonna carry all this stuff?"

"We'll try."

"Can't we just stop at places on the way?" Dawson asked.

"We can. But chapter six says never assume there are supplies out there. I mean, what if there are gangs that claimed them. Then we go tromping out without food and starve. No, we need to leave now and with supplies. We wait any longer we're gonna need a boat."

Dawson smiled.

"What?"

Dawson gabbed Judd's hand and led him to the back kitchen window.

"What?"

"Why don't we take that?"

Judd peered out the window. Two doors down, in a neighbor's back driveway was a boat, it was about twenty feet long and covered, already on a trailer attached to the truck.

"I was joking about the boat."

"We should take it just in case."

"Dawson, I really don't think ..." Judd looked up when the thunder clapped loudly and the ground vibrated. "Yeah, maybe that's not such a bad idea. You know, just in case."

"What about gas?"

"I don't know. We'll figure it out. Hopefully he'll have gassed it up."

"Enough to get to Branson?"

"Probably not. Wait... that's not Mr. Westerman's yard is it?"

"Yeah, it is..."

"Shoot. Well, he probably washed away by now. Let's go see if we can find the keys."

"Should we bring the stuff with us?"

"We'll wait until we pull it in front of the house. But we have to go out there now."

"Want me to stay here?"

"No, you'll come with me. Do you have a coat?"

Dawson hurried to the living room closet, he pulled out a rain coat and his rain boats.

To Judd he just looked so cute all dressed in the blue plastic wear. He took a hooded jacket and placed it on. It wasn't going to matter, he was going to get drenched. At least Dawson would stay semi dry. Judd had avoided one thing though, looking out or opening the door.

When he did, sure enough, Tire Man was still there.

"Why is he here? Maybe he's hungry," Dawson said. "Like a stray cat."

Judd took Dawson's hand and never taking his eyes off of Tire Man he stepped off the porch. The water covered his shoes, along with ankles, and came to Dawson's lower shin. He took a few steps and stopped.

Something was wrong. He looked left and right.

"What is it?" Dawson shouted over the downpour noise.

"The water is moving. The book says not to go out with moving water." He looked all around. It moved like a stream but it was a flat area, no slopes. It didn't make sense.

Clutching Dawson's hand they moved faster, they had to make it across the lawn, avoiding Tire Man who didn't move. As they made it from Dawson's yard, he then noticed the street. The water wasn't running one direction. It was going back and forth, unnatural looking.

A few more steps, the ground vibrated and the water moved faster. Then Judd felt a strong jolt, it nearly knocked him from his feet. He stopped walking when the water began to disappear,

"What the heck?"

Another tremendous jolt hit as if someone dropped a heavy object beneath his feet, and before he could register what was happening, not only did the ground crack, it split, separated wide and a huge chunk dropped, taking Dawson with it.

"Judd!"

Judd was still holding his hand and had to lower to the ground to keep his grip on the child.

Dawson balanced on a slab of concrete, his one hand joined with Judd's.

"Hang on!" Judd hollered. He couldn't see anything below Dawson, he didn't know how far down it went. Judd panicked, he begged in his mind to not lose Dawson. However the rain made it impossible and slippery. He struggled to pull him, losing his footing. Dawson tried to climb, but slipped back.

"No!" Judd pulled. "Please." The rain fell against his face and the grip he had on Dawson was slipping.

"Don't let me fall! Don't let me fall!"

"Try to climb." Judd grunted pulling harder.

He had Dawson's wrist, then his hands, then fingers ... until finally, a sickening feeling hit his gut when Judd realized he was going to lose him.

His little fingers slipped from his and Judd cried out, ready to dive in, but before Dawson could fall into the hole, he was hoisted upward, gripped by his little rain coat and set on the ground next to Judd by Tire Man.

Shaking and on the verge of tears from fear and horror of what could have happened, Judd grabbed on to Dawson, grunting outward in desperation and wrapped him tightly in his arms. "I'm sorry. I'm sorry."

He wasn't letting go. Not for a second, even with the rain coming down.

Judd had to calm down, he couldn't move. His whole body spasmed out of control. On the ground he took a moment, squeezed Dawson tighter and looked up to Tire Man with gratitude.

NINETEEN – FULL HOUSE

The couch was comfortable. Morgan had propped pillows behind her back and was able to sleep without too much pain. In fact, after she had fallen asleep, she didn't wake up like she had the previous night. Then again, her injuries were still fresh.

Ross was a good man, a family man. He had been with his wife his entire adult life and they waited awhile before having children. His job as a police officer and his wife not wanting to put her public relations job on hold to have a family caused problems early on in their marriage. They worked it out with the help, he claimed, from God, family and their church.

Morgan wasn't real big on the 'God" thing.

Ross picked up on that and shook his head when she was dismissive.

She was quickly learning a lot about Ross, one thing she realized was they were going to butt heads, and often. They were both hard headed people and their journey ahead was going to be interesting. The difference between them was she was more heated and he seemed a lot more even keeled.

They actually got into her life, too. How her husband left her for a woman with children, when he was the one that didn't want them.

He started doing some counselor, long term married man bullshit to her and she cut him off.

"I wanted him to stay, he didn't want to." Morgan blasted.

"Marriage is not fifty-fifty, it's a hundred percent on both parts." Ross stated with passion.

"Really?" she snapped. "So his cheating was my fault too." Seriously?

"No 'one' person is completely innocent." Ross insisted.

"Oh, that's so not true. That is such male shit." Morgan stated dismissively.

"No," he said, shaking his head. "This is coming from someone who was cheated on."

"Okay, so why is this important now?" Morgan asked. "He's dead."

"That's cold." Ross said shaking his head.

"It's true."

"You don't feel loss over a man you shared your life with?"

"No! I felt loss when he left me for her," Morgan said irritated. "I grieved. Now I'm relieved, so it's not important. The problem is now over and finished."

"You still need to forgive him."

Morgan laughed. "What for?"

"You'll carry this the rest of your life. Plus, I am sure his soul could use it."

"I don't care about his soul. Not now and I don't want to forgive. Come on, you've been there. How long did it take you to forgive?"

"Not long."

"Then you're a better person than me. If I need to forgive I will, but not now. It's a moot point."

"Are you in pain?" he asked, changing the subject, or so she thought.

"No. Why?"

"You're being very snippy, or is this just because of the radio call?"

The radio call? Morgan thought about it for a bit.

Actually, it did set her off, or rather Ross' take on it.

They both were overwhelmed when they heard it and despondent when they were unable to reply.

The man on the radio simply called out. His call number, his location and asked if anyone was there. Three times he repeated his call and then he added a, "I received a message and have information I need to share about an extinction event," then he gave a specific date that a pilgrimage to life would leave Branson. It was in one week. It was urgent, the man said, that all come to Branson.

That was it.

Yet something so basic was a source of contention between them.

Morgan saw it as a man who had information too in depth to give over the airways, so he simplified it with urgency. Pretty simple, Morgan believed, it was a join me message.

Ross on the other had delved deeper into the simplistic message. He believed the message was somehow more spiritual.

Again, Morgan laughed. "I hate to think of what the extinction event is. I mean, what does he call most people dropping dead? Think maybe he's in touch with a scientist or something?"

"I don't know," Ross said. "I think you were right in believing there may be pockets of places with people."

"So you don't think it's a God thing."

"Oh, I think it's a God thing." Ross nodded emphatically

"Ross, you are a cop. I can't believe you are thinking this way. Blaming God is a cop out. You are going to feel awfully silly when you're wrong." Morgan said dramatically.

"Won't you feel silly when you are," Ross said a bit irritated.

"Um, it will take the skies opening up or Jesus himself making an appearance for me to believe this was something other than one that has a scientific explanation."

They agreed to disagree on that aspect, but did find themselves in agreement on leaving. They would head towards Branson and give it their best shot at getting there. A man called out on the radio, it was one more survivor in the world, and they wanted to find people. Survival in the aftermath would be better if they joined, or formed a community.

They planned to leave in the morning.

Morgan knew life on the road wasn't going to be easy and she self medicated and slept.

Ross must have spotted her open eyes.

She smelled the coffee.

"Made you a cup and filled a thermos," he said.

"Thank you."

"You might want to fill your belly."

"What time is it?"

"Almost noon."

Morgan started to sit up and then groaned. "Why did you let me sleep that long?"

"You needed to rest. Are you still in pain?"

"I'll know more after my body works out the kinks," she said. "I'm nowhere near the pain I was in yesterday."

"Good, Good. You need your strength and wits about you. In fact, we need to figure out some things out. We have a problem."

After telling her that, Morgan grabbed the coffee and took a big drink. Then another. The coffee helped her 'wits' and she stood from the couch and followed him across the lobby. "What's going on?" she asked.

Ross walked to the automatic doors. "I shut them down. Take a look."

She didn't really see anything through the slightly tinted glass, and the SUV along with canopy over the driveway blocked her view some. As soon as she joined him at the door, she saw the problem and gasped.

Outside of the motel, in the parking lot and not far from the door were people. Like the ones back at Ross' house, they just stood there staring, only difference was, this time instead of a dozen, there were hundreds.

TWENTY – ONWARD

It took a while for Judd to get it together. He felt like an utter failure. He nearly lost Dawson. Granted there was no way for him to know the street would break, but then again, had he paid any attention to the warning signs in the book, he wouldn't have gone further.

Moving water means danger.

Still, Dawson fell down that hole and had it not been for the heroism of the mute Tire Man, Dawson would have died.

Judd wasn't sure Tire Man understood what he did exactly. After setting down Dawson, the big guy stepped back. Judd didn't know how to react. He still didn't trust Tire Man, hero or not. Something was missing in his eyes. A soul, a conscious, something. No matter how good the dead, Judd wouldn't allow himself to trust him. He nodded a thank you, but then after embracing Dawson, he hurried through the rain to get to Mr. Westerman's house to get the truck and boat. Dawson didn't say much, just 'thanks and wow you're cool'. Judd didn't tell him that it was Tire Man that pulled him out. He would, just not now.

Judd felt a little silly getting the boat. After all, it was just rain, and really, where would they be going that it would get so flooded that they'd need to float their way to Branson?

However, something inside of Judd told him they needed the boat, it wouldn't hurt. If they didn't need it and were wasting gas, then he'd simply ditch it. If they did end up needing it, at least Judd knew how to man it.

He was right. The rain had washed away the gross remnants of Mr. Westerman and his lawnmower incident. All that remained was his lower torso and left arm. Apparently, Mr. Westerman was going on a fishing trip. The twenty foot, aluminum motor boat was secure on its trailer and hitched to the Chevy four by four.

A cooler was in the back of the truck, but it wasn't full. The fishing gear was in there, but the keys were not.

They had to find them.

"You okay buddy?" Judd asked. "Wanna just stay near the garage and I'll check the house?"

"You should check Mr. Westerman."

"I am not checking Mr. Westerman. Besides, there's nothing left."

"You have his legs." Dawson corrected him.

"Just stay put," Judd told him and walked into the basement door.

Dawson didn't listen, he followed.

"Does he have a wife?" Judd asked. "Just wanting to be prepared. You know, for another body."

"No. He lived alone."

"Good."

"Except when his son came over, then he wasn't alone. But I don't see his son's car."

"Just help me look for the keys."

"I still say …" Dawson stopped speaking.

"What? What's wrong?"

"Listen. It stopped raining."

Judd lifted his head, peering up to the ceiling. He didn't hear the rain. The faint sound of rolling thunder was still present, but for the time being, it had stopped pouring down.

As if he weren't in debate enough about the boat, the lack of rain made Judd really wonder if they should take such a gas hog as the truck.

He pushed forward on the search, they checked everywhere. Every place in the house. They did find the boat key. All by itself on a ring with a keychain from Bruce's boats.

No truck key.

"Try Mr. Westerman," Dawson kept saying.

Finally, Judd relented and said, "Fine. I'll try Mr. Westerman."

"Want me to?" Dawson offered.

"No!" Judd snapped. "Why aren't you traumatized, you fell in a sink hole?"

"Because you saved me. I feel really safe with you."

Judd groaned out a swell, and was at least grateful it wasn't raining. He headed back outside to check Mr. Westerman, or what was left of him.

They exited the house back out the basement door. Judd was a little surprised that their shadow, Tire Man wasn't anywhere around.

He looked up to the sky, it was still overcast with dark gray storm clouds. He walked toward the back yard and stopped at the edge of the grass staring out to Mr. Westerman's remains.

"Go on. Go check," Dawson said.

"Shush," Judd told him. 'Have some respect."

"Should we pray for him?"

"No, I don't think that's gonna help."

The yard wasn't huge and the back portion of it was at a slight slope. That was where Mr. Westerman's remains were.

There was about six inches of water that flooded the yard. Not enough to cover the body. First step into the yard, the ground vibrated. Judd without hesitation, grabbed hold of Dawson's hand.

"I'm fine."

"I'm not taking a chance."

"Are you going to make me come with you?"

"Just stay close. Don't look. It's pretty bad," Judd said.

"You should have seen it when the mower was running."

Cautiously, holding Dawson's hand super tight, he walked across the yard.

He knew immediately why Dawson squealed out an 'ew'. A part of Mr. Westerman's hand was all by itself a good ten feet from the other remains. Probably tossed aside when he was getting chopped up.

The closer he got he could see a bit of shredded shirt, a few bones, and what remained of Mr. Westerman's torso. It was mowed clean.

"Hopefully, he didn't have the key in his shirt pocket," Dawson said. "Should we check the grass."

"If it's in the grass we won't see it with all the water."

Judd cringed both facially and internally. He hated, really hated that he actually was going to check the lower remains of Mr. Westerman. Was it worth it? Did they really need to take that boat? What it they just found that Bruce's Boat place?

He was there, right there by the pair of legs, buttocks up, covered in what probably was green pants. The pants were soaked from the water, and the waste was semi blood stained.

Mr. Westerman still wore a belt.

"Okay, here it goes," Judd said, crouching down.

He wanted to gag, throw up, in fact his stomach churned. From above the waist of Mr. Westerman's pants extended a shredded part of his abdomen and spine.

"Oh my God," Judd groaned out.

"What?"

"This is horrible."

"Does he smell."

"Yeah, he smells."

"I can't smell him."

"Trust me, he smells."

"What's he smell like?"

"Dawson," Judd said with a correcting tone. "All right, here I go." Holding his breathe, Judd reached out and aimed for the back pocket. He stopped when Dawson screamed. "What?" he asked the boy.

"You're touching him."

"I have to touch him if I want to look for the keys. Okay, I won't go in his back pocket. I'll feel." He patted the back pocket area, then looked over his shoulder when he heard Dawson snicker. "What now?"

"You're touching his butt."

"Stop. Frist screaming and now laughing." He exhaled in frustration. "Okay no keys there. I'll check the front packet." He slid his hand under the torso. "No comments, please." He reached into the front pocket, paused when Dawson giggled and then Judd smiled.

He lifted the keys.

"See. See?" Dawson said with glee. "I told you. Didn't I?"

"You were right." Judd stood up.

"Now what?" Dawson asked. "We leaving?"

Judd looked up at the sky. If the rain held off, they could wait around to leave. But was it a chance he wanted to take?

"Yeah, let's head back to the house. Finish getting what we need and we'll head out."

Dawson nodded. "Should I get in the truck?"

"Yes, we'll drive it to your house. That will make it easier to pack."

Dawson walked toward the truck.

"Wait," Judd said. "How old was Mr. Westerman?"

"Can't you tell?"

"No." Judd snapped. "I can't judge someone's age by their legs. Unless you know, they're a woman. Even then, there are some older women with legs that …" he cleared his throat. "No I can't tell."

"Why do you need to know?"

"I just do."

"Old."

"Like how old? My age old, your dad's age old …"

"You and my dad are the same age. He was grandpa old."

Judd winked. "Then I think we need to see what all Mr. Westerman has before we leave. If he's grandfather old, then he didn't rely on technology as much. Bet he has maps and all sorts of stuff we can use."

He didn't want to get into it with Dawson, what all he wanted to search for, because Judd himself, didn't quite know. He just knew that when he searched Dawson's house, there was nothing useful. Not a power tool or even a map. Not that Judd was a survivalist, but that book had quite the list and before they left, he wanted to check Mr. Westerman's house for some of those items Dawson's parents didn't have.

TWENTY-ONE – CONCERT OF ARMS

Following the letter of the law, Ross went outside to have a smoke, that was when he saw the crowd. He didn't notice them at first. It was early, he was half asleep and in his own world. He looked down only at the ground and didn't peer beyond the truck until he wanted to see the rain.

There was something about the crowd of people that struck him as scary. They all looked the same, stared the same way as if operating on one brain.

They could get out, get in the truck and drive right through them, but was that the right thing to do?

He wanted Morgan's opinion. He made her coffee, woke her up and broke the news. Figuring if she were like his wife, she was easier to deal with and more clear headed after a few sips of coffee.

She looked out the front door for a while. "How long have they been out there?"

"They've been there since I got up," Ross replied.

"Have they moved?"

"Not once."

"Okay, we get in the truck and drive through them."

"Morgan, they're people. Living breathing people."

"If I'm not mistaken, didn't one of those people try to kill you?" she asked.

"Not them, Tanner did. He was a violent person before. We don't know anything about the people standing there. They may feel pain, know what's going on and not be able to do anything about it."

"Not our problem. If we want out of here and they don't move, just run over them."

"Jesus, you're cold."

"What do you want me to say?" she asked. "If you don't want to do that, then we stay put. We stay until we go. We can walk, I don't want to walk. We have a perfectly good vehicle out here with gas. So we can stay and they will eventually leave or make their way in."

It would be a different story if every end of the world book and movie were right. If those people out there looked like creatures or were undead. They weren't. They looked normal, like people in the morning waiting on the subway.

Ross decided to check the back of the motel. If it was a free and clear escape, then they could find another car. The back was surrounded as well. One big circle of the staring people encompassed the motel.

The rain came down steady and hard and not one of them moved an inch.

Morgan made the decision for them both to wait. Wait until they left. Even if it delayed them a day, Branson was a thousand miles west. They could do that easily. They had gas to get half way.

After the decision to wait was made, not an hour later, the crowd moved forward. They pressed against the window, hands and finger tips squeaking as they ran down the glass.

None of the people out there showed violence. They hadn't tried to break through, but that didn't mean they wouldn't.

It was Ross' turn to make the executive decision. Most of their items were already in the truck. They merely had to shoulder the bags they brought in.

They would try to go.

Morgan was agreeable.

The front double doors were blocked and their best option was the exit at the far end of the first-floor hallway. Go out that door and make their way through the people to the SUV. Then he thought about Morgan. While she presented tough, she still wasn't well.

She cringed in pain quite a bit and knowing broken ribs, she wasn't in shape to make it through a mob of people.

What if they turned at any second and became violent?

There was no way Morgan could fight them off.

By the elevator was an emergency fire case with an extinguisher and ax, Ross broke the glass on the case and took the ax. He placed only one bag over his shoulder and left the other two, along with the radio, in the lobby with Morgan.

"Just wait here. I'll bring the truck in."

"You're going to crash through the window?"

"That's the only way."

"I can go out there with you," She said.

"No. I can't take that chance."

"They're not moving out of your way. If you intend on driving through the front window, you'll have to plow through them."

"I don't have a choice. At this rate, they'll be in the building and we'll be barricaded in a room. No, this is the only way. Stay here and wait."

It was good in theory. Walk out, squeeze through the people, get in the truck and drive into the lobby. That was until Ross went outside.

His last encounter with the seemingly zoned out people ended with one of them having a death grip on his jaw. Ross had a small ax and nearly a fully clip in his revolver to make his way through hundreds of people.

He didn't know what their reaction would be. Would he even make it through them? He would use any of his weapons if he needed to.

As prepared as he could be, ax in one hand, gun in the other, Ross opened the emergency exit door, at the end of the west wing, of the first floor. Mentally, he envisioned himself pushing through the people and to the truck.

He didn't expect so many blocking his way.

In his mind if he didn't speak to them, or try to communicate, it would be fine. He figured that was the reason Tanner snapped, Ross had talked to him and made eye contact.

The second he stepped outside, he lowered his head and moved onward. At first it was like a rock concert full of people, pushing his way through annoying individuals who didn't budge. How many times had he done that in his life and career.

Moving through hordes of people focused only on themselves. Only instead of booze, these one smelled really bad. The odor of urine and feces filled the air blending with a moldy water smell, it was so rank, his glands swelled and mouth salivated from the gag reflex.

While they seemed to be standing still, they weren't. They moved forward toward the building and the instant Ross opened that exit door, one of them grabbed for it, trying to keep it open.

"Oh, no you don't," Ross said and shoved the man aside, blocking the door until it closed again. He didn't need them rushing in.

Mistake.

It wasn't just eye contact or talking, Ross quickly learned physical contact made them 'awaken' and the man who reached for the door suddenly focused on Ross.

His arm shot up and he grabbed on to Ross' shirt.

'Okay I can do this,' Ross told himself and forged forward.

His shirt was held tight and the collar of it pressed against his throat with every step, choking him. He twisted and jarred his body to get free, only to have another move into him, then another.

If he were claustrophobic, Ross would have been in a panic. Suddenly he was mobbed.

One man holding his shirt, while the others moved into him, squeezing against him.

He could feel their hands on his body, fingers grabbing and scratching.

They were still people, they were still human. Don't hurt them, he kept repeating in his mind. It was useless. Each step was blocked and Ross found himself buried in the crowd. It was hard to breathe, hard to move.

Hands grabbed for him, bodies pressed against him, each step he took was harder than the last. Within a minute his face was pressed against other faces and he found himself in nothing less than a human vice.

Ross couldn't breathe.

As much as he didn't want to desecrate life, it became a fight to live.

The human walls were closing in. He was literally being squeezed to death.

It was time to fight back.

Just slipping through was no longer an option.

He hated to do it, but the moment someone's fingers dug deep into his flesh, along with the burning pain, Ross screamed out and swung the ax.

He didn't want to use his ammunition, so he kept swinging. It seemed futile. His hacking didn't make a dent. Those squeezing the life out of him didn't even notice. Ross had to amp it up a notch.

The SUV wasn't that far, yet the weight of the people were holding him back.

Not only did they compress him, they struck him. He felt the blows of pain to his legs, mid-section, head and chest,

With war cries flowing from him, he swung back and forth, in and out.

He pushed his way around to the front of the building. He could barely see the SUV. So many people surrounded him blocking Ross from getting to the SUV. He moved against the grain, feeling not only the lack of air, but the burning as his flesh took the brunt of their kicks and scratches.

He envisioned himself as a football player, plowing through them all. The one man still held onto his shirt.

As he neared the front of the building, Ross not only swung the ax, he flung his body, fighting his way through until he reached the SUV.

He opened the driver's door and Ross finally pulled his weapon. He shot the man that grasped his shirt, then Ross slipped inside and turned over the engine.

He was injured. He knew he was bleeding, yet couldn't let it stop him. He put the SUV in reverse and backed up. He shuddered when he heard the thuds against the vehicle.

After a quick turn of the wheel, he shifted the car in drive and slammed on the gas. Driving through people wasn't as easy as it seemed. They rolled from the front end of his car and got caught under his wheel.

The SUV bounced as it ran over the people and Ross not only heard the crunch of bones, he could feel it too. He felt it physically and he felt it in his soul. Every person he killed, he absorbed emotionally.

Eventually, he broke free and rammed right in and through the front lobby window,

Morgan was waiting with the bags and as soon as the truck was clear enough, she jumped in.

"I was worried," she said.

"I'm fine."

"You're hurt."

"I'm fine," he repeated. "I'll worry about it when we're clear."

"What's going on with all these people, Ross?"

"I don't know. I wish I did, but I just don't know." Quickly, he shifted the SUV in reverse and prepared for the bounced, thump and thud of human lives falling beneath the wheels off his vehicle.

He never wanted to run them over, or kill them. Ross had no choice. It was what he had to do to get him and Morgan away and safe.

Ross knew, even making it out of the motel parking lot wasn't the end of it all. More obstacles would lie ahead.

If getting out of the hotel was that difficult, he didn't want to think about how hard it was going to be to get to Branson, Missouri.

TWENTY-TWO – CHASING RAINBOWS

When Dawson was seven, to celebrate his First Holy Communion, he went to Idlewild Park in Pennsylvania with his best friend Sawyer and his family. They left on a Friday and they got to miss school. Dawson's mom and dad didn't go and it was the first time ever, Dawson had been away from them.

His parents were at work when they left for the park, they had said their goodbyes and gave kisses when they left for the office. Mr. Westerman came to the house to see Dawson off.

Dawson likened that day to his leaving with Judd. His parents weren't there, he looked back to the house several times as they drove down the street. Mr. Westerman was the last person he saw ... sort of. There were a couple differences. There was no best friend, just Judd, he rode front seat in a pickup, and Mr. Westerman didn't give a long list of instructions.

Mr. Westerman, did however, give a lot of other things.

Judd had taken a tool box and two of those orange gas cans. Mr. Westerman had fishing gear, a bunch of maps, and some old looking thing Judd called a CB.

Judd kept in on the floor of the pickup right under where the change holder was.

Dawson played with it a lot that first half hour of the trip, and even though Judd had it plugged in, it wasn't working.

"Maybe it's old," Dawson suggested.

"There's just no one chattering," Judd said,

"Does it need the internet?"

"No, buddy."

"It's strange."

"I wrote a song about one of these things," Judd said.

"Was it any good?"

"Not really, I liked it. No one really made a fuss about it. It was a cut on one of my albums."

"How did it go?" Dawson asked.

"Let me think." Judd tapped the steering wheel a few times, hummed, then snapped his finger. "It was a while ago. The chorus went something like this ..." he sang the word. "Been around the world, never looking back, now I can't go forward a single step. You rocked my heart, you rocked my world. I see you, you see me, when I'm away, there's always the CB."

"You sing good."

"Thanks."

"I can see why people didn't like it." Dawson looked out the window. He was glad it stopped raining. The sun wasn't out and it was going to be awhile before the water dried up. That was if it didn't rain again.

'Objects in the mirror are closer than they appear' was written in the bottom of the passenger's mirror. Dawson didn't get it, why put a mirror on a car that wasn't accurate.

Through that mirror he also saw Tire Man sitting in the bed of the truck.

"Why'd you bring him?" Dawson asked. "I thought you were scared of him."

"I am."

"Then why'd you bring him?'

"You saw him, Buddy. He was trying to get in." Judd shrugged. "I figured maybe we can train him like you suggested."

"If he don't die from the cold and rain. My mom always said, I'd catch my death of cold playing in the rain."

"All mothers say that."

"So it's not true? Did my mom tell a fib?" Dawson asked.

"No. It's sort of true. You catch a cold and you can die."

"So, Chuck the Tire Man is gonna get rained on and catch his death of cold. That's a mean thing to do to him. If you wanna train him you have to keep him alive."

"Aside from being scared of him, he doesn't smell all that good. Maybe the rain will wash the smell away."

"If he doesn't die from it."

"I got news for you. Our Tire Man... he hasn't drank water or eaten anything from what I've seen. Pretty much, that's what's gonna kill him."

"That just seems wrong." Dawson glanced out to the mirror again. Tire Man sat against the side of the truck, his head was turned to the back watching the road go by.

"Wanna play a road game?" Judd asked,

"What's that?"

"Different games you play to make the miles go faster. Some we can't play because there aren't any cars on the road. Well there are, just not enough."

"Sure." Dawson said.

He was surprised they were driving as well as they were. At first he thought they'd never get out of the city, but Judd zig zigged through back streets and was smart about it.

"Go," Judd said.

"What?"

"Go first."

"And do what?"

"You weren't listening were you?" Judd asked.

Dawson shook his head.

"Sorry. I'm sorry. You're probably finally upset about everything. I mean you were pretty cool back home with Mr. Westerman and that hole. I was the mess there. You were brave about falling."

"That's because you had me. I don't know how you did it," Dawson said. "You were fast, too. I felt your hand let go and next thing I know you are swopping me out of that hole like Superman."

Dawson saw it. Judd looked away and stopped smiling.

"Dawson, I have to tell you something."

"What is it?"

"I dropped you. Not on purpose. My fingers slipped, they were wet."

"But you got me."

Judd shook his head. 'No, he did." He pointed back.

"What?"

"Soon as I lost grip, Tire Man was there and plucked you out of the hole so fast I didn't have time to register it."

"Wait. Why would you lie to me?" Dawson asked.

"About what?"

"You let me think it was you."

"I never said it was me. I just …. I just figured I'd tell you when we had time. I'm sorry. Don't be mad."

"Did you at least say thank you to Tire Man?"

"Yeah, I guess," Judd said.

"Is that why you brought him? So he can save me again?"

"No." Judd shook his head. "I brought him because he wanted to come and after what he did, it was only right."

"Stop the truck."

"Why? Do you have to pee?"

"Stop the truck, please, Mr. Heston."

"Mr. Heston? This is serious."

"You said call you that when it counts. I want this request to count. Can you stop?"

"Sure thing." Judd slowed down and then after stopping put the truck in park.

Dawson reached down to the small gym bag on the floor and unzipped it.

"What are you doing?" Judd asked.

After setting a bottle of water and one of those premade peanut butter sandwiches on the seat, Dawson opened the door. 'I'll be right back."

"Dawson?' Judd opened his door.

It was a tough climb down. Dawson had to stand on that little ledge by the door and slide to the ground, he reached up and grabbed the sandwich and water. By the time he was on the ground, Judd was there.

"What's going on?" Judd asked.

"He may smell too bad to be in the truck and he may not even be safe, but he saved my life Judd. The least I can do is try to save his."

"Humbled," Judd said. "Good idea."

Dawson walked to the back of the tuck. Tire Man was much higher so Judd lifted him up. "Here you go. I know you're hungry. Try to eat." Dawson said to Tire Man.

Tire Man didn't take the water, it dropped into the truck, but he did manage to take the wrapped peanut butter sandwich. Expressionless he looked at the sandwich.

Judd set Dawson down.

Tire Man put the sandwich to his mouth, wrapper and all.

"No. No" Judd reached out. "Let me open that for you." The second his hand was near the sandwich, Tire Man released this soft but scary growl and his eyes darted at Judd.

Judd quickly pulled back his hand and stared. "Let's go, Dawson."

"Boy he must be hungry."

"Yeah." Judd said inching Dawson along. "He must be."

Instead of waiting for Dawson to walk and get back into his side, Judd lifted him and placed him in the truck and shut the door. He watched in the side mirror as Judd walked around the back of the truck only pausing to look at Tire Man.

It wasn't long and they were back on the road driving.

TWENTY-THREE – ROLL BY

It bothered Ross and Morgan knew it. His face was bruised, his arms had gashes, he looked as if he had been beaten by a mob. When in fact, in a sense, he had been. They didn't reach out and hit him, bite or scratch him, instead they acted like a boa constrictor and tried to squeeze him in. It was the fight to get through that caused the injuries. Those would heal, his mind would take longer.

The tough officer of the law was affected when he dealt with the people that moved outside the motel. So much so, that not five miles down the road and free and clear of the mob, Ross pulled over, stepped from the SUV and walked to the side of the road to vomit.

"Are you all right?" Morgan asked.

With his back to her, Ross lifted a hand but stayed at a distance. Morgan took the time to review the map and compare it to her weather charts. She opened up the back hatch and spread them out, taking cover from the rain under the lifted back end.

They were still in Pennsylvania, but not far from the Ohio turnpike. Even with accidents and cars off the road during the drop, they should still be able to make it free and clear through the highway, provided weather didn't hinder them.

It had rained steadily, but slowed down to a constant drizzle when they were leaving the hotel.

Basically, they fled the motel and just jumped the nearest highway going west. Fortunately, it was the right direction.

She was chilled and looked at the map for a possible stopping point to get clothes and a jacket. It was spring and the temperature didn't surprise her. It worried her, rain could turn into snow. Considering one inch of rain was about a foot of snow, they were in trouble if the temperature dropped any more.

Sipping a bottle of water, Ross approached. "Figure out anything?" he asked.

"Yeah, we could take this route pretty much to Akron then catch another highway. I'm worried about the weather."

"How so?"

"When I looked up the weather maps back in the city, this is what I printed." She pulled out two sheets of paper and lay them side by side. "This one is the jet stream. Weather moves from west to east and typically follows jet streams. As of that day, the jet streams were coming from Chicago, down into Ohio and east. The national weather operates on a color coded system. For storms. Light blue to red and harshest can be white or black. This light color here west of Akron," She pointed. "Pale blue. This is what we are getting right now. Light rain. That darker color, red, we're running right into. That hit Akron last night, this morning, it's not as bad as what just hit Pittsburgh. I'm guessing." She pointed to a weather system just before Akron.

"So we missed it."

"That one. This one here is the one I am worried about. It's big and blackened out. Not a printing error. This should be about a hundred miles west of Akron, and it's bad. We'll hit it late tonight if we keep going. Then again, I'm making predictions on this. Everything is one big storm system, just pockets of intensity."

"How did you learn to predict weather."

"I watched it constantly," Morgan said. "I was obsessed especially when they called for snow. I got so tired of them being wrong, I started learning it."

"Did it help?"

Morgan nodded. "Yes, when I was wrong, I could only blame myself."

"So, Miss Weather Gal, what do you suggest?"

"Hit Youngstown and head south instead of heading due west. Try to miss it like the one we missed in Pittsburgh. It's one o'clock now, we can go a few more hours and then find a safe place to hunker down."

"Then that's what we'll do."

Morgan folded the papers. "We also need to figure out a way to get gas, we have some just not enough to get to Branson."

"We'll figure it out." Ross reached up for the hatch.

"Are you better now?"

"Somewhat."

"Was it because you ran over those people?"

Ross facially winced. "Yes, Morgan. I ran over those people and got sick about it. It bothered me. Didn't it bother you?"

"I don't see them as people."

"How can you say that? They're living, they're breathing..."

"They're dangerous. Maybe one or two aren't, but they operate like animals in a pack mentality. What one does the others do. At least from what I saw at the motel. If we don't figure out a way to get through them, we're in trouble if we run into too many of them. They won't give a shit if we feel bad."

"Were you always like this?" Ross asked, shutting the hatch.

"Like what?"

"Mean. Hard."

Morgan stared at him for a moment, then headed back to the passenger's door. "No. Not always."

"Just wondering. One more thing..."

Morgan stopped.

"This storm you're talking about. You used the term hunker down. How bad is it?"

"I don't know. I never experienced it ever. Red usually is tornado weather. Hopefully we'll avoid it, be under it, but we still need to hunker down," she said. "Put it this way, I believe if there are survivors in that area west, God help them. Because if they aren't ready, there probably won't be survivors when this storm is done."

TWENTY-FOUR – DASHING MEMORIES

Dawson gave the queerest of looks to Judd when he they passed a road sign that read 'Lodi' and Judd chuckled out with fond remembrance. "Oh man, Lodi. Bet you love Lodi."

"I don't think so," Dawson said after staring at Judd for a moment or two. What's Lodi?"

"Wait. You don't know Lodi, Ohio. Little dude, that's only like forty miles from you. You never were in Lodi?"

Dawson shook his head.

"Man, how have you not been to Lodi. Even I was in Lodi and it's not so small they call it a village."

"Like with huts?"

Judd laughed. "No. There's a whole string of small towns west of Akron, all following the same route."

"You're not from around here. How do you know?"

"Back in the day, we moved around quite a bit on a tour bus. About ten years ago, we were headed from a concert in Erie to Columbus. Passed through the small towns and the bus broke down right outside of Lodi. In fact, we pulled off the exit hoping to find a car repair place and we just busted down. Squad car came by to help out. Just so happened we couldn't get a mechanic if we tried. It was the Sweet Corn festival they have. Just ..." Judd noticed Dawson was staring out the window. "I'm boring you, aren't I?"

"No." He paused. "Yeah, a little."

"Lodi is a cool town."

"Hey, maybe the small towns are saved. Maybe they're so small they didn't get hit."

"Maybe," Judd said.

"Like Branson. It isn't big. I dreamt of it you know."

"You told me."

"Some guy named Bill was waving his arm at me saying, 'Come to Branson'. "

"You didn't tell me that."

"What do you suppose it means?"

"It means we should go to Branson."

"Think we should stop at these small towns and look for people?"

Judd took a moment to think about it. While they were supposed to head south west before Lodi, they could continue west, even for a little bit, to check the towns. It wouldn't take them too far from the route and it would be worth it to look. All around them was desolation, chances were small town or not, it would be the same way there, too. Besides, what would it hurt to look?

TWENTY-FIVE - SPOT

The planned route outside of Youngstown, Ohio came to an unexpected end when the road entered what looked like a lake just west of the town of Canfield.

It went across too far and wide to see.

"Did we just hit the end of the country?" Ross asked. "Is everything flooded from here on in? This is insane."

"That's ridiculous."

"Seriously?" Ross snapped. "Are you calling me ridiculous?

"No, just your idea. It has to be the small lake a mile north of here." Morgan looked at the map. "We'll back track and just head further south."

Ross didn't think that was going to work. He swore that somehow the three lakes north of them spilled over from all the rain, if that was even possible. But his fears were unfounded and they remained on dry land.

The name of the town, Salem, sent chills through Ross. He even suggested they go around it. However, the Super Center at the edge of town was calling even him.

The parking lot was full of cars, only a few had crashed. Decomposing bodies scattered about the blacktop. They had a bloated look to them, even more so than other bodies Ross had seen. He attributed it to the rain.

It was dark when they entered the store, no power, the further back in the store Ross went the darker it was. He was able to find flashlights and lanterns. His main search was for those things. Batteries, a Coleman stove, survival items.

Perhaps even some food items.

He was shocked when he saw that Morgan had grabbed a heavy winter coat from the clearance rack.

"It's April," he told her.

"I'm being prepared for snow."

Ross laughed.

"Go on, laugh. It's not even fifty out there. Any colder all that rain is going to be snow. Then we're in trouble."

Ross paused. "Did you see any men's coats?"

They remained in the Super Center probably longer than they should have. Ross had gotten them enough supplies to 'hunker' down as Morgan put it for the night somewhere.

They decided that after Salem, they go about a hundred miles or so southwest and start looking for a stopping place. The weather was holding up, the rain tapered, and Ross held high hopes that Morgan was wrong about the weather front.

They loaded the truck and took the main road toward town. Riding shot gun, Morgan checked the map for alternate roads to get through, figuring, even though smaller, they'd run into the same.

Cars blocking the roads, making things impossible.

There wasn't much conversation in the SUV. In fact Ross found himself increasingly annoyed with Morgan. He once had a partner that annoyed the hell out of him and he used to joke to him, "Man, I swear you're my purgatory. The world ends I'm gonna be stuck with someone like you."

He was kidding.

Morgan was worse than that partner and here Ross was, traveling with the only other person that was alive and lucid and he didn't like her. How did that happen? What did he do in his life to have that?

Bad weather, earthquakes, Ross started feeling silly for wanting to stop, find a quiet corner and get 'me' time. Who does that at the end of the world. Ross was patient and tolerant and all that was going out the window.

His fleeting daydreams of ditching her came to a halt when he stopped the SUV. Ross smiled.

"What is it?" Morgan asked, her nose buried in a map. "Do we need to back up?"

"No. Life."

"What?" Morgan lifted her head. "Oh my God." She, too finally smiled.

Not far ahead, a few blocks perhaps, when the quaint town square of Salem began, they saw people.

They moved across the street, on the sidewalks, pushing strollers and even saw what appeared to be a man walking a dog.

Ross drove faster.

"Careful, they probably aren't expecting a car to come down."

"Yeah, you're right." Ross slowed down. Maybe it was the east side of the country. Maybe it wasn't a dead world after all.

The ecstatic grin on Ross' face took a nosedive when he saw the man walking a dog. He held a lease, but the dog wasn't walking. He dragged the decaying carcass of the animal along the sidewalk.

He looked quickly to Morgan when he heard the 'click' of the automatic locks. The moment the SUV came to a stop, so did everyone in town.

As if all automated, every single person halted and slowly turned at the same time to face the SUV.

"Back up?" Morgan suggested.

"Yeah, backing up." Ross put the SUV in gear and turned his body to peer out the window. When he did he saw more behind them. "Shit."

Every second they waited more came, hundreds of them and they slowly made their way to the SUV. There were far too many, too close, that plowing through was going to be impossible.

TWENTY-SIX – NUN OF THAT

Judd supposed he should have known, Wadsworth and Seville were both a repeat of what they had seen only on a smaller scale. The biggest difference was the ability to make it through main roads. There were vehicles that collided and some had gone off road. They even saw a car that had hit the steps of the Seville Methodist church and flipped over against the doors.

Nothing was hopeful.

At one point, Judd actually thought, *"Wow, if we keep going further, I'll need to use the boat.'*

Water started to rise around Seville, coming mid rims of the tires. It subsided after a mile.

When they approached the interchange to get on Interstate 71, Judd contemplated forgoing Lodi.

What was the use.

However the optimist in him, the one who wanted to find life, along with Dawson's insistence, Judd stayed on the route road and drove to Lodi.

He remembered that road well, the same one he took into Lodi years ago. The same one his bus broke down on.

He recalled the story to Dawson hoping he could catch his attention on it. It was a good story, he broke down, the corn festival and the band that cancelled.

"We ended up playing for them." Judd said.

"Were they happy?" Dawson asked.

"Wish I could say they were. It was like a round of gulf claps when we were done. Some old guy walked up to me and told me to keep trying. Funny." He shook his head and then eased on the breaks. There was a line, four wide of stopped cars. Some smashed into fender benders, some not.

Not far beyond that, on the small crest of the road right before the village of Lodi, lay an overturned tractor trailer.

"How odd is this?" Judd asked. "This is where the bus broke down."

"How do you know?"

"The funeral home. I remember sending Pat our stage manager over there to see if he could get help." Judd opened the truck door and stepped out. He walked around to Dawson's door and opened it. "Wanna walk in town and check?" he asked. "It's not too much further."

"I don't know. I don't like seeing bodies. If it's like that last place they're all water logged from the rain."

"Yeah, but it's a nice day, kind of chilly though. Why don't you step out, take a leak and stretch your legs." He helped him out of the cab of the truck. When he sat his feet on the road, Judd saw his guitar in the back and pulled it out.

"You playing now?" Dawson asked.

"Feeling nostalgic."

"Not sure what that means," Dawson said walking slightly away to do his business.

"Stay where I can see you," Judd said. "Nostalgic means sentimental, looking back at the past and it makes you happy and want to relive it."

"So if I went to Cedar Point I would be nostalgic."

"Yep." Judd strummed the strings, tuning his guitar.

"Honestly, Judd, I don't get why playing your guitar on a road full of abandoned cars would bring back good memories."

"Oh!" Judd blasted out. "Oh my God, you saw that old movie, too."

"What?" Dawson came out from behind a car.

"What was it?" Judd waved his hand, trying to jar his own memory and snapped his fingers. "Guitar, highway ... Stand."

"I am."

"No, the movie, The Stand."

"Never heard of it."

"It was a while ago, way before your time, actually my time. But it's classic. Super cool show based on a book by Stephen King."

"Who?"

Judd waved out his hand. "Anyhow, the book is about a sickness that kills everyone." He climbed up the front fender and sat on the hood of the truck.

"Like now."

"Sort of. Anyhow ... Oh man, it's like prophetic ..." he paused. "That means he predicted this. Like Stephen King was psychic or something. Plague, sickness, everyone drops dead. So this rock and roll guy, Larry has a guitar."

"Like you," Dawson said.

"Sort of. I'm country and better looking." Judd winked. "Anyhow, Larry is like all alone, going nuts, he stops on a highway full of abandoned cars ..."

"Like this."

"Exactly. He gets up on a hood of car like this and started playing a song on his guitar. Middle of a song, a boy comes along ..."

"Like me!" Dawson said.

"And a woman."

"Was the song like magic?" Dawson asked.

"Nah, but it was a freaking iconic scene."

"Why don't you play it and see if a woman comes?"

Judd laughed. "Okay." He fumbled the chords at first, trying to remember the pattern, then he had it. He played with intensity, graveling his voice in a mimic of the made for television movie he remembered so fondly.

He swore he was doing well, too. It felt right and the words were sadistically meaningful at the moment. He was going strong until he noticed he didn't have Dawson's attention anymore.

"Man, you are a tough crowd." Judd slowed down his playing. "What are you doing?"

"Where are the people?"

Judd sang. "It happened on a sunny day ... the wind blew and took all life away ... you may not hear a breath or single sound, that's because no one else is around ..." He shook his head with a chuckle. "Man that was good for off the cuff, wasn't it."

"For serious, Mr. Heston. Where are they?"

"What do you mean?"

"If they all dropped dead and crashed their cars ... where are the bodies?"

"Huh?"

"They're all gone," Dawson said.

"Don't stop!" A female voice called out in the distance. "Please don't stop playing."

Dawson, wide eyes hurriedly looked at Judd. "The magic song brought a woman." He then pointed.

Judd slid from the hood of the truck, putting his guitar over to his back and stepped forward.

"You heard the lady, play," Dawson said.

It was an odd request but Judd brought his guitar around and strummed the chords to the song. He did for just a minute and stopped in shock when he saw the woman.

She made her way around the overturned semi and moved between a walk and a run their way. It wasn't a survivor in blue jeans and a half buttoned down blouse in a state of shock. She was happy to see them.

He couldn't tell her age at a distance, but she didn't look old. Actually, she looked too young to be wearing the uniform.

The simple white colored shirt underneath the navy jumper style, plain dress and the cross she wore, threw Judd off.

She wore one of those headdresses, too. A short one rested more to the back of her head. Judd saw that when she approached.

Judd was the one in shock.

She smiled. She had a naturally beautiful face. Out of breath she approached and immediately crouched down to Dawson and embraced him. "A healthy child." During her embrace she glowed with a grin and extended her hand to Judd.

"I can't tell you how happy I am to see you two. I'm Sister Helena."

Nervously, Judd touched and then shook her hand. He was speechless. He didn't expect to see anyone alive, let alone a nun.

Her story would be interesting.

TWENTY-SEVEN – CONSCIENCE

"Go." Morgan slammed her hand on the dashboard. "Go. Go, Go. Now."

Hand gripping the gear shift, Ross looked forward. There were many, too many at the hood of his SUV. He peered in the rearview mirror, they were at the back gate, too.

What there was of the daylight was fast blocked out by the people that mobbed the car.

"What the hell, go." Morgan yelled.

Beads of sweat formed on his top lip. He didn't see monsters when he looked out. There were no sores, no decaying flesh. In fact the only marks on them were injuries probably from falling or from a car accident.

These people had a soul, they were alive. They were just suffering and confused.

The last place they went Ross plowed through about four and it filled his gut with guilt. Now, not only were there more of them to go through, he could see their eyes.

"Ross, what are you waiting for?" Morgan demanded.

Suddenly Ross saw him. He stood barely making it over the hood. A child about ten years old. He stood next to a woman wearing a fast food uniform, the left side of her face was burned.

"I don't think they'll hurt us," Ross said. "Let's wait. See if they leave."

"They aren't leaving. Go through them."

He shifted his eyes to Morgan. "I can't. I can't do it. I'm gonna make a run for it."

"No!" she screamed. "Why would you do that? Hit the fucking gas and go."

Ross shook his head. "No. I don't have it in me to kill them. I know it sounds weak ..."

"Sounds weak? It is weak!" Morgan reached over.

"What are you doing?

"I'll drive."

"Stop it." He pushed her hands form the wheel. "I honestly don't think they'll hurt us. Just open the door and make a run for it."

"We have supplies."

"We'll get more."

"You're insane. This is what will cause our death. They are out there. They aren't human like we know."

"No, Morgan, they aren't. But that doesn't give us the right to kill them."

"Yeah, it does," Morgan said. "It's us or them. Choose us."

Ross was prepared to argue. He truly believed that if they waited, they would go away.

He was wrong.

Just as he opened his mouth to speak, he saw the man with a baseball bat aiming for Morgan's window.

"Morgan! Watch out ..."

Crash!

The baseball bat smashed the passenger's window and slipped from his hand, through the broken window into her lap.

Morgan screamed. Arms reached in, grabbing for her blindly, while she fought their grip.

"Ross! Get them off!"

Ross reached over and grabbed the bat, trying to get them from her, but his swing was limited in the vehicle.

"Run them ... over," she ordered.

He put the SUV in gear, but too many blocked the vehicle, he couldn't move it.

"It won't go."

"You did this!" she blasted, they grunted as they pulled her hair and she turned left to right in her seat.

Ross' insides shook, overwhelmed with a wave of feeling like a failure, Morgan screaming out, Ross reached for his door.

Bat in hand he pushed it open and when it did he noticed everyone had moved to the right front side. No one was on his side, they all crowded the front and passenger side.

He would have to clobber his way through to get to her and free her. He was just about to do that and he stopped.

Not a single one of them was in his way or even near him. They went after Morgan.

He had his escape, his way out, his diversion.

With those thoughts, Ross didn't run to help Morgan, he ran the other way.

However, a mere fifty feet away, he stopped again.

What the hell was he doing?

As much as he didn't like her, she was in that position because he didn't want to take a life. Yet, he was willing to sacrifice hers. It had nothing to do with fear. At that moment, when he chose to run, it was them, him or her and he chose himself.

A decision, he knew, if he continued on, he wouldn't be able to live with himself.

It might have been to late or futile, but still holding the bat, Ross raced back to the SUV.

TWENTY-EIGHT – HOLY INFORMATION

She looked uninjured and in great shape and to Judd she was pleasant enough, unlike the stories he had heard about nuns. But in the five minutes he had met her, he was really close to telling her, "Step back a little, Sister." Because instantly she grabbed on to Dawson's hand and wouldn't let go. Keeping him close as they walked. Maybe Judd was making too much out of it but it seemed to him that through her actions she was almost saying, she was better qualified to watch out for Dawson.

Sister Helena wasn't fazed by Tire Man in the back of the truck, she did eye up the boat without scoffing, then asked Judd to follow her. Judd grabbed his main back pack and went with her. Tire Man never moved.

"You're a God send," she told him.

"I wouldn't say that," Judd replied as they walked toward the town of Lodi.

"I would. I was praying for help and then I heard you singing."

"You need help?" Judd asked.

She nodded. "Well, not me, personally. Father Basko."

"Wow, I have been to this town. I didn't know it had a big Catholic employee population."

She smiled. "You're funny." Then she looked down to Dawson. "He's funny."

"Mr. Heston is nice," Dawson said. "He's been taking care of me."

"Heston?" She tilted her head. "What a wonderful name. I'll take that as a sign as well."

"What's wrong with Father Basko?" Judd asked.

"We stopped here for the night, to rest up for our journey. Get supplies and he was injured."

"I'm not real good with medical stuff," Judd said. "I'm not sure how I can help."

"You're bigger and stronger than me. You can help," she said.

"Where are you traveling from?"

"Erie," she answered. "We have been hitting towns along the way. Looking for survivors. Especially when we got the message."

Judd stopped walking. "From God?"

"No. No." She smiled. "A man on the radio back in Erie. We've been fortunate enough to dodge the deadly weather, but any more delays we won't be."

Judd looked around, he was near center town of Lodi, and it hadn't changed at all. His eyes were locked on the gazebo in the town square.

"Mr. Heston?" she called him.

Judd snapped out of his day dream.

"This way." She pointed to the building with the sign, 'Lodi Village Office' across the street. "Please."

As they cross the street, Judd noticed a short yellow school bus parked outside, he didn't think much of why it was there, he followed Sister Helena.

"We were staying here. It was easy."

"There's a drug store," Judd said, giving a nod of his head to the large chain drug store a block away. "Were you able to get supplies there to help?"

"That's not the type of help I need." She opened the door. "This way."

They walked through a small reception area, and that was when she finally released Dawson's hand.

Dawson stopped in the middle of the room. He looked around. "How many people are with you?"

Judd found it curious that the child would ask that, then he noticed the sleeping bags, the leftover food on the table.

"Please," she beckoned and disappeared into the back office. "Father, I found help."

Judd looked at Dawson then stepped forward.

"Judd," Dawson whispered.

"What?"

"Don't make me hold her hand anymore."

Judd winked and mussed his hair, then walked into the office.

He expected to see the priest, maybe on a couch or something. He didn't expect to see him lying on the floor, pinned underneath a huge shelf. His face was black and blue and his eyes were puffy. To Judd he looked like he had taken a hell of a beating.

"Oh my God," Judd rushed to him. "How long has he been like this?"

"Since late last night," she answered. "I couldn't move it."

"Can you help him, Judd?" Dawson asked.

"Gonna try." Judd crouched down to the older priest. "Father, can you hear me?"

Father Basko coughed and nodded. "Yes, thank you. Thank you for coming."

"I'm going to try to lift this," Judd said. "Then we'll get you off the floor. Does anything hurt?"

"My chest. I can't breathe well."

Judd examined the shelf, it was about six feet tall, thick and cherry oak. The contents of the shelf were on the floor around Father Basko. They were probably the reason for his bruised face. They more than likely fell on him. It was going to be tricky. If Judd could get it high enough, he could use his back to push it up against the wall.

He knew it would be heavy, Judd didn't think it would weigh as much as it did. On his first attempt, he lifted it a few inches causing Father Basko to cry out when he levered it up, and then again when he lowered it back down.

"Sister, I am going to move this up. You are gonna have to slide him out. Father?" Judd asked. "Can you move your legs?"

With a pained expression, Father Basko nodded. "Yes."

"She's gonna grab you under your arms and pull, if you can shift your body scoot her way. Okay?"

"Yes." He nodded.

"Ready, Sister?"

Sister Helena scurried around to Father's head and placed her hands under his back.

"Wait," Dawson called out. "You're doing it wrong!"

Judd paused. He was at the top of the shelf. "What do you mean?"

"You're trying to lift it upright. Just lift it from the side and flip it. There's room. Flip it."

"Dawson, that's a great idea, buddy." Judd moved his position to the side. He nodded to Sister Helena and while it wasn't any easier or lighter to lift, he was able to use the weight of the shelf to tip and tilt. He held it there until Helena freed Father Basko. Once the priest was clear, unable to flip it entirely, Judd let it fall back to the floor.

Father Basko cried out in pain.

"Did you get medication from the drug store?" Judd asked. "Pain stuff?"

Sister Helena shook her head no.

"Let's get him to the couch, you stay with him and I'll see what I can get."

"We don't have time," she said. "We have to keep moving."

"There is no medical attention around here. We're it." Judd said. "We can't move him. Not yet."

"We don't have time."

"All we have is time." Judd said. "Dawson, give me a hand with the Father."

"What do you need me to do?" Dawson asked.

"Clear the couch." He looked down to the priest. "Can you handle it if I help you up? It's only a few feet to the couch."

"I'll manage."

Judd braced under Father's Basko's arms and lifted him. He knew it hurt the priest, he could tell by the way his body tensed and Father Basko fought back grunting in pain. Sister Helena helped get him to the couch.

Once he was settled, Judd leaned down. "Father, I am not a doctor. I have a book in my bag that tells me how to do basic First Aid and stuff, but I need your help. When I was nine, my father took me to this fishing spot. Man, it was a long hike. I fell. I felt really bad. It was a long way back and my dad asked me to know my body. What was wrong. That way he could gauge. So I am asking you to tell me what I need to focus on. What is happening with you that needs fixed."

"My sternum," he answered with labored breath. "My ankle."

"Okay, I'll see if I can find stuff over at the drug store. I'll be back. I'll get you pain medicine, too. You allergic to anything?"

He shook his head no.

Judd stood up. "Come on Dawson, come with me." He paused and looked at the shelf. "How does something like this happen?" Judd asked. "It's too big to fall on its own."

"It was a terrible accident," Sister Helena answered.

"It was no accident," Father Basko said.

"It was an accident." She reiterated.

"No, it wasn't!" Father Basko insisted.

Judd whistled. "Okay, Sister did you do this to him?"

"What?" she said in shock. "No."

"Dawson said it looked like others were here. Were others with you?" Judd asked. "You said you were looking for survivors."

"We were," she replied.

"You found no one?"

"Oh, there are many out there. They just are heading west and wouldn't travel with us."

"Neither should you," Father Basko said. "You and the boy go. Don't let our burden be yours."

"What's going on?" Judd asked.

"You and I. We think alike." Sister Helena said. "Father Basko disagrees."

"Sister, I don't want to be rude, but I don't know what you're talking about," Judd said.

"This way." After touching Father Basko's arm, telling him she'd be back, she walked from the office.

Judd and Dawson followed her.

She continued outside and pointed to the bus. "You have a man in the back of your truck. Why?"

Judd looked to Dawson first. "He wanted to come. He saved Dawson's life."

"You see a human being in him, right?" she asked. "To you he's not dangerous."

"Right now. Yeah."

"Yes, well, I can't see danger either. I can't leave them. They'd die without me."

Judd was about to ask her to clarify, but she kept looking at the bus. Instead of asking, he walked to the open door.

"Judd, don't," Dawson said. "I got a bad feeling."

"It'll be fine. Stay here." Judd walked up the first step and into the bus. When she brought up Tire Man, Judd pretty much expected to see a couple people like Tire Man in the bus, what he didn't expect to see were children.

About a dozen of them sat on the bus, all different ages. They sat there staring forward, until they noticed him and all of them, at the same time, looked his way. They stared at him, just watching, not moving.

Judd stood there a moment, which was as long as he could stand to. Looking at them all, a chill shot through his spine. To him it was freaky. They were children, yet something about them scared the hell out of him. Judd left the bus immediately.

TWENTY-NINE – REGRET

What was Ross thinking? He wasn't a coward. He never ran from problems. In fact, he was the guy on the force they said never thought of himself when running into dangerous situations. Yet, there he was, beating the pavement racing, it was a good two blocks before he stopped, turned around and ran back.

The distance was short, however the guilt he carried weighed him down. All he could see was the SUV and the mob that completely engulfed it. They weren't flesh eating creatures, but they were dangerous in a way Ross didn't understand.

Morgan had likened them to a boa constrictor, pressing and squeezing their victims. Ross didn't figure out the why of it. Maybe they just wanted to eliminate what they thought was a threat.

At the moment it was Morgan.

Was his distain towards her so bad that he chose to let her die rather than deal with her? Instantly he became the bad guy, no matter what he did in the past, or would do in the future, leaving her forever defined him.

He raged toward the mob, wielding the bat, swinging it to get through. None of them paid attention. A few fell from the hits, but he didn't make a dent. He powerhouse blow was delivered with emotion and guilt.

Like the regrets the mobbing people weren't going away.

Finally he realized he couldn't do it. He was down. Defeated. He alone was responsible for the death of the only other living person.

Arms and back aching, chest heavy with emotions and breathing labored, Ross dropped the bat and walked backwards. He turned when he was far enough away from the SUV, placed his hand on his knees, bent over slightly and caught his breath.

There was a tap on his back.

He stood straight, and turned around.

Morgan stood there.

"Oh my God," he gushed out,

"You son of a bitch," she said with words deep and gutsy.

Ross wasn't expecting it, and barely saw it coming. The moment she spoke she swung out the bat and connected it to him.

It was lights out.

<><><><>

Morgan didn't hesitate. There were no regrets or guilt. Not a single smidgeon of her conscience was bothered by it. After nailing Ross, she left him. On the street, not far from the SUV and the mob of depraved people.

She didn't give him a second thought. Morgan was enraged.

How dare he?

There she was, fighting for her life, those ... things grabbing for her, pulling her hair. She was injured, her ribs still hurt badly. Yet, Ross took a couple pitiful swings in the truck, then opened his door.

She thought he was coming to help her and in her mind that was dumb, because the second he flew out, she was released enough to scurry to his door and get out.

Once she made it outside of the vehicle, she knew he wasn't coming to save her, he was running and leaving her to die.

She stood for a moment in shock.

He left her? He just ran and left her.

In that few seconds she really justified what he did. Maybe he was scared, thought she was dead. Then it hit her that he was a coward and he just left her all alone and Morgan became livid. How dare he abandon her! She moved toward the closest building.

She thought about running after him, then he turned around to run back.

Even those actions didn't stifle her anger, it fueled her emotions. He came back after the fact, when guilt hit him. She charged his way to verbally attack him, blast him for what he did, and then she saw him drop the bat.

That bastard.

She grabbed it and as he faced her, she hit him hard. Not knowing if he was dead or alive, or even caring, Morgan left him. Unlike Ross, she left him in the road, without a second thought and didn't care if those things to get him. He deserved it.

THIRTY – FOUND

"Can we just go, please," Dawson asked as he stayed close to Judd, walking to the drug store, not far from where they left the sister and priest. He moved fast, probably faster than he should have. "I don't want to be here. I want to leave."

"I know, Buddy."

"How did that shelf fall on him?"

"I don't know."

"You heard him, he was scared. Never knew a priest to be scared like that."

Judd stopped when they entered. "It's a new world, none of this ever happened. Of course, he's scared. We're all a little scared."

"Yeah, but he doesn't look like he watched a scary movie scared, he looks like he's living scared."

"That's perceptive. Pharmacy is back there." Judd pointed. "Why don't you look around for things."

"No. No way. I'm staying right by you."

"That's fine, too." Judd led the way.

"I want to go. Let's go back to the truck and just leave. Please."

"Dawson, we have to help the priest. Come on, I saw that Catholic school uniform. I would think you'd want to help the priest."

"No, I didn't like the priest at our school. Besides…we can get him his pills and whatever else you want, then can we go. Please, can we just leave?"

"You just want to leave them?"

"You heard her," Dawson said. "She wants to leave now. Get her the stuff and she'll leave."

"Well maybe we help her and all leave together. We still have a lot of daylight left and we …"

"No!" Dawson snapped. "No, you seen them Trancer kids, right? They're bad. I need to get away from the Trancer kids."

"Trancer?" Judd asked.

"My name for them. Because they look like they're in a trance."

Closed mouth, Judd bobbed his head from side to side. "That's a good name for them. Easier to say, 'look out there's a Trancer'."

"Yes, and we need to look out," Dawson said. "I got a bad feeling. Made my stomach flop. More than Tire Man. I think we should leave him, too."

"Whoa, Whoa. Wait," Judd held up his hand. "Not an hour ago you were feeding him a peanut butter and jelly sandwiches. Now you want to ditch him?"

"That's because an hour ago, he was by himself. What if they work like dumb animals? Like they do whatever the others do."

Judd walked behind the pharmacy counter. He grabbed a flashlight and looked at bottles. "I didn't think of that."

'Ever see the movie Village of the Damned?"

Judd laughed. "Yeah, and I can't believe you did."

"I didn't want to, yet I did. O was torn. All those kids had like a bug in them and when they were together they worked like one brain."

"I assure you this is not the case," Judd said.

"How do you know?"

"Because this isn't sci-fi shit, or aliens, this is … nature." His hand moved about as he talked. "Something that caused people to drop dead, it didn't kill everyone, the ones it partially affected are your … Trancers. Probably brain damage. We haven't seen anything to make us think they're dangerous."

"Liar."

"What the hell, Dawson." Judd shook his head and then smiled when he found a bottle of pain pills. "This will work." He faced Dawson. "Why'd you call me a liar?"

"Cause you saw something in Tire Man. I saw your face."

"He just acted weird when I reached for his food."

"Like an animal," Dawson said. "Please."

"Tell you what. I feel bad leaving that nun alone with all those kids and the priest, but you are my priority. If you look me in the eyes and tell me to leave and do so after we give them the pills and bandages, we will."

"Which eye?" Dawson asked.

"What?"

"I can only look in one eyes at a time."

"Wow that is so cool you asked that. They say when you look in a person's left eye your lying. So the right please."

Dawson focused on Judd's right eye. "I won't feel bad, it's the right thing to do, let's leave after you give them the stuff."

"Then we will." Judd rubbed Dawson's head. "Let's finish up and go."

Dawson exhaled a breath of relief that moved his entire body. He felt better, but that didn't stop him from continuously looking behind him.

<><><><>

The trip to the drug store was a good thing and not just for medication. It was food for the soul. Dawson took a bag and loaded it with candy. Judd thought smarter, granola, crackers, juice, stuff like that. Not Dawson, he didn't even get normal candy. He picked the stuff that old people usually ate. Butterscotch and chewy gummy candies.

He moved a lot more lighter and upbeat as if the weight of the world was off his shoulders.

The more Judd thought about it, the more he liked the idea of just him and Dawson on the road.

"Thinking about it," Judd said as they walked. "We got about seven hundred and some miles to Branson. If we hit a decent amount today, like a couple hundred, stop for the night, we'll hit Branson by tomorrow."

"You think anyone is in Branson?" Dawson asked.

"I don't know. But it looks cool, right?" Judd asked.

"It does." Dawson agreed.

"And it's a goal. Something like this, we need a goal."

"What happens if no one is there?"

Judd shrugged. "Then we pick another goal. Sadly, the world is ours. We can do what we want, right."

"We don't know that. There might be people on the other side of the country."

"True. There might be. We just ..." Judd noticed Dawson stopped cold at the school bus.

"Hey, pal," Judd put his hand on Dawson's back. He looked up quickly saw the kids all staring out the windows, hands against the glass, then he looked away. "Don't worry about them, okay? We won't be with them."

Slowly, without saying a word Dawson lifted his arm and pointed.

"What? What's wrong?" Then Judd saw. He didn't at first. In the middle of the short bus, staring out the window, was Tire Man.

"He joined them," Dawson said. "See?"

"I see we just got a guilt free way of leaving Tire Man behind. Let's go,"

While Judd projected confidence, he wasn't. The sight of Tire Man on the bus with the kids ... scared the hell out of him.

<><><><>

"No!" Dawson screamed out. It was the first time that he acted in a temper tantrum manner.

Judd pulled him aside. "Little man, come on."

"You promised. You promised."

"We are still leaving," Judd then dropped his voice to a whisper. "We're not traveling with the kids. I promise you that."

Dawson shifted his eyes to Sister Helena. She held on to Father Basko, supporting him around the waist.

They returned from the store and handed over the medicine, then Judd helped clean up and bandage Father Basko. Dawson was alright with that, until Sister Helena said. "I'll drive the bus. Can he ride in the back of your truck? He can't sit up. He has to lay flat."

He saw the look on Judd's face. He was caving in. Judd was a 'yes' man who couldn't say 'no'.

So Dawson did. At first, he was calm and even tried to be mature. "No, Sister we're leaving."

Sister Helena smiled politely. "We all are."

"No," Dawson said. "We're leaving alone."

"Mr. Heston?" She looked at Judd.

Judd cleared his throat. "Sister, we have a destination and we kind of want to get going."

Sister Helena chuckled in disbelief. "You made me wait. I wanted to leave, get him help at another stop, but you asked me to wait until you got the medication."

"Now he is fit to travel," Judd said. "He wasn't before."

"Please." She stepped to him and grabbed his hands. "Please don't leave me to do this alone. I will if I have to. We are all survivors in this. We should be together."

Judd relented and Dawson freaked out.

"Let them go," Father Dawson said kindly. "Sister, let them leave. I'll be fine here."

"No you won't," she looked at him. "You know what's coming."

"Not for certain. The child is frightened and rightfully so. I'm frightened. I'll stay. Take those ... children and do what you need to do."

Judd held up his hand. "Father, you aren't well enough to be alone. Let me talk to Dawson, I'm sure he just doesn't understand ..."

"Oh, he understands," Father Basko said. "Probably better than you. Probably better than us all. Whether you believe it is fate or God, either way, there is a reason those of us who survived, did, and are together the way we are. You and he are partners."

In his mind, Dawson whined an "Aw" then huffed a little. "Fine. Fine." He quickly tried to change his brash behavior. "It's okay. He can ride with us in the back. It ain't him anyhow."

Suddenly, Sister Helena looked hurt. Her expression dropped.

Dawson held up his hand. "It's not you Sister Helena. It's not. You seem nice. It's the kids in the bus. Ever been bullied? I have. You see a bully and you know it's coming. I see those kids and know it's coming." He grabbed Judd's hand. "Let's go get the truck."

Father Basko lay his hand on Dawson's head. "Thank you."

"Just don't tell me to confess. I hate confession. I didn't like having to go. Since we don't have school anymore I wanted to say that."

Judd smiled as he looked down at him, told Father Basko and the Sister they'd be back and they left the main street of Lodi to get the truck. They had to drive around the Semi to get into town, it took about fifteen minutes.

When they returned, they took cushions from the couches in the administration building, placed Father Basko in the back, and then using the tarp from the boat they created a tent over the back in case it rained.

And it did. Not hard, but a steady drizzle.

The last thing Dawson remembered was Judd telling him as long as they moved slowly, they could keep going on the highway until dark.

The steady rain coupled with the rhythm of the moving truck, and with the fact he hadn't slept much, made him tired. He started dozing off and on while Judd talked, then Dawson propped his head against the truck passenger door and fell asleep.

Until the truck slowing down and stopping was like an alarm clock.

He was dreaming again about that guy named Bill in Branson, waving his arm, yelling "Come to Branson." He wanted to look at the brochure to see if Bill was on it, maybe that was why he was dreaming of the strange man.

He thought that too, in his dream until he woke and sat up with a start.

"Why are we stopping? What's wrong?" Dawson asked.

Judd pointed.

Dawson couldn't see over the dashboard, but Judd opened his door. "Judd!"

Once Judd stepped out, Dawson did the same. He climbed down and by the time he walked around the truck he saw why Judd stopped.

A woman walked towards them. She held her side, her brown hair was pulled into a pony tail, she looked beat up like Father Basko, but she smiled as she looked at Judd.

Dawson hurried and ran around and caught up to Judd just as he approached her.

"Thank God," she said. "I ran out of gas. There's nothing around. I didn't think I'd see another person" She looked at Dawson and smiled. "Hey there."

"Hey." Dawson lifted his hand. She looked harmless.

"Can I ride with you?" she asked. "I have my own supplies." Her eyes shifted. "Is that a nun driving that bus?"

"Yep. Sure is," Judd said. "And ..." he looked at Dawson. "Is it okay she come with us? Or do you want her to ride on the bus? Or perhaps you want to leave her behind?"

"Can't leave her behind. Jeez, you make me sound bad," Dawson said. "She can ride with us. Besides the bus is too crowded anyhow."

Her eyes widened. "That many people?"

Dawson grumbled. "If you wanna call them that."

"What?" she asked, confused.

Judd waved out his hand. "I'm sure he'll tell you all about it in the truck. Come on. Do you need help with your stuff?"

"No, I'll get it. It's just a backpack." She moved quickly, even with a limp, to her car. She grabbed a backpack and returned.

"You been alone?" Judd asked. "Seen anyone else?"

She paused. "No. No one. I've been alone."

"I'm Judd and this is Dawson."

"Nice to meet you. Thank you again. I won't be a bother." She held out her hand. "Morgan. My name is Morgan."

THIRTY-ONE – COPE

The pain was intense from his cheekbone to his temple. That was where Ross took the hit. He saw it coming and couldn't react. Morgan nailed him so hard, he literally saw stars and then nothing.

He deserved it.

It didn't matter what kind of person she was, leaving her behind to die was *not* the kind of person Ross was.

He was still on the street, trying to make it through the pain. He lay on the ground in a semi-curled position. He moved his head slightly to press his aching cheek to the damp and cold ground. It felt good. His face was swollen, he could feel the pressure against his eye. Ross moved his hand to feel his face and in doing so, his hand hit something. He widened his fingers to feel.

It was a foot.

Ross opened his eyes.

He was surrounded, all he could see were legs. They encompassed him, dozens of feet were almost pressing on his body.

In a panic he sat up and took a foot to the chest. He wheezed out and struggled to stand. He believed if he stood he wasn't at their mercy, he was wrong.

The second he stood upright, they moved closer.

He could feel the weight of bodies against him, inching his way, closing in the circle. The air was thick and a feeling of claustrophobia hit him.

Ross couldn't move. Not forward, nor back.

There was no way out.

This was it for him, the end.

A serving of Karma for what he had done.

Ross tried to be brave and figure a way out. He pushed and shoved, but they sprung back with more force. How many were surrounding him? He could barely see over their heads and even then, it was only a sea of people.

Where did they all come from?

Every moment that passed, he found it harder to breathe.

They were literally squeezing the life out of him. He was in a human coffin.

However, this was his life, not theirs to take.

If Ross was going to die, he wanted to control when he passed.

It took everything he had to reach his shoulder harness and pull out his pistol. His range of motion to his arms was short. Keeping the pistol close to his chest, he engaged the weapon while looking at those around him.

There was a young man in his twenties, an older woman wearing a waitress uniform, a police officer, none of them really looked at him. They stared blankly and through him.

It wouldn't be long, Ross knew, before they crushed him completely.

With a struggling grunt, he put the gun under his chin.

Painfully he closed his eyes and thought of his wife, his daughters. How badly he missed and loved them and how he would see them soon.

His finger trembled as he put pressure on the trigger.

Waitress woman moved against him, and Ross proved once again to himself that he was a coward.

He couldn't do it. He couldn't take his own life.

Quickly he moved the gun, put it under Waitress woman's chin and fired.

Her head flung back from the force of the shot, but she was held up by the mob and didn't fall.

She was a standing corpse, balancing on the weight of those around her.

Ross' adrenaline pumped, his heart beat out of control. He moved his body so he could aim and fire again.

Crying out with frustration and the will to live, Ross kept firing until the clip was empty. By then he had created a small opening and he shoved his way through. His arms swung, legs kicked and he forged ahead with the momentum of his body until he broke free. He tripped over someone's legs and fell to the ground hard.

Peering over his shoulder, Ross saw them turn, visually targeting him and moved his way.

He would not be trapped again. He stumbled to a stand, looking back only once.

The SUV was there, abandoned by the horde and Ross rushed that way. The driver's door was open and he jumped inside. The keys were in the ignition, in fact the engine was still running. He had never shut it off, only put it in gear.

He peered in the rear-view mirror and only then was he able to see the magnitude of the amount of those who pursued him. It wasn't a dozens, it was hundreds. Ross placed the SUV in drive and peeled out.

Once he was free of the mob, he slowed down enough to look around town.

He didn't see any sign of Morgan. After circling around a few blocks, he headed out of town and back to the main road.

Ross was a plethora of emotions.

He was guilt ridden over what he had done to Morgan, ashamed of his actions and angry at his weakness. Two times in two days he had the gun under his chin ready to take his own life.

Truth was, even with his overwhelming loss, he wasn't ready to die. He didn't want to die.

The world had perished around him and he was spared. There had to be meaning to having life when do many others perished. He was a fool for not seeing it, and he needed to honor it going forward.

Life was a gift. He fought physically to keep his and vowed he would never take being alive for granted again.

There was a plan in motion before they even pulled into the town. A plan to go west. Alone or not, Ross was going to stick to that plan and head to Branson, Missouri.

THIRTY-TWO – FIGURE

The new woman, Morgan didn't say much. She sat in the back, sleeping most of the time. The main highway, while not free and clear was easy to maneuver for about eighty miles, then the weather took a turn. Almost instantly the sky darkened and the temperature dropped. The rain increased in intensity until it began to hail.

They had to stop and bring Father Basko into the truck. It was far more dangerous in the back than it was for his body to sit up.

That was when Morgan woke up.

She helped Judd with Father Basko, then Dawson sat in the back with her.

Before they pulled back on the road, Judd noticed Sister Helena had stepped from the bus. Before he got back in the truck, he went back to see what was going on.

"How much further?" she asked. "We are going to need sturdy shelter before nightfall. The weather is only going to get worse."

"All weather comes from the west, so we're gonna run into it. Maybe head south after Dayton and pull over?" Judd suggested.

She nodded, wiping the water from her face. "I'm good on gas until then, you?"

"Good. I'll lead the way, stay close, the roads will be slick."

"I will, thanks." Arms folded to her body, she hurried back to the bus and Judd went to the truck.

"Okay," he said as they got inside. "We're gonna keep going until right after Dayton and pull over." He grabbed the map from the floor and tossed it to Dawson. "Take a look and see where we can stop."

"Want me to look?" Morgan asked.

"Nah, he's good." Judd looked in the rearview mirror, then pulled out.

"Is everything alright with Sister Helena?" Father Basko asked.

"Yeah, she just wanted to know when we were stopping. The weather is getting bad."

Father Basko shifted in his seat. "I worry. She is not seeing clearly. She's following her faith and not her heart. Sometimes ... you have to draw a line."

"It's hard to do in this situation," Judd said. "I mean, people are people and it's hard to see beyond the fact that they are alive."

"I disagree," Morgan said. "Out there, I don't know if you ran into them, but there are people out there that are not alive. They're shells and soulless, and I can see the distinction."

"Wait until you see what's on the bus," Dawson said. "She has a whole busload. At least twelve."

"Oh my God," Morgan looked out the window. "In the bus she's driving?"

Judd nodded.

Father Basko slumped in the seat toward the door, he reached over and touched Judd's hand. "Promise me you won't let them in the shelter with us. Don't let them in under any circumstances."

"I'll make that promise," Morgan interjected. "I know what the Starers are like."

"Starers?" Judd asked.

"That's what I call them."

"I call them Trancers," Dawson said.

"Trancers, Starers," Judd shook his head once. "Man, you people have really cool names for them. Why haven't I thought of one. How about you Father? You have a name for them?"

"Yes, I do." Father Basko raised his eyes to Judd. "The Abominated."

<><><><>

Columbus, Ohio was gone. Not geographically displaced, but rather it was destroyed. What caused its demise was anybody's guess. The skyline was dark, the buildings that had not been reduced to rubble were mere support beam skeletons of their former shapes. Debris of wood, concrete and glass scattered everywhere, and sections of town had been burnt black. There were no fires smoldering, the weather battled the flames and won. There had been a lot of rain, so much that it caused the river to overflow and spill across the area, covering the land and hiding the roadways.

The beltway around the city was nearly as dangerous. Trees and branches strewed across the expressway and several inches of water glazed the surface. So much so, they took a longer route.

It was in Columbus that Morgan began adamantly suggesting that they lose the boat.

"We're not losing the boat," Judd said.

"It's weighing us down, making travel difficult, plus eating a lot of gas."

"We're not losing the boat," Judd repeated.

"We need the boat," Dawson said.

Morgan laughed. "You need the boat? Why? Are you gonna go fishing?"

"Hey, now," Judd said. "Don't make fun. He says he needs it, so we take the boat."

Groggily, Father Basko joined the conversation. "We're going to need the boat."

A slight jolt went through Judd when he heard the father say that. "Why do you think we need the boat?" Judd asked Father Basko.

"When we were in Cleveland, just before the earthquake hit, we were communicating on the radio. There was a man with us, Steven, he was killed in the quake. Anyhow, there are two more storm fronts coming. They were described to us as looking like huge land hurricanes. Two of them joined together. They're gonna dump a lot of rain. We're driving right into them. We can go north, south, doesn't matter, they're that big."

"How is that possible?" Judd asked. "How is any of this linked? I mean, the weather, the people …"

Father Basko shook his head with a groan. "I don't know. The information we got was relayed, this person said that, and so forth. We didn't get all the details. We hoped we would, but everything shut down communication wise. Sister Helena and Steve got the last message. I was sleeping. She knows a bit more. They were kind of theorizing it was a manmade thing. Weather, atmosphere manipulation gone bad."

"Oh, balls," Judd scoffed. "That isn't possible."

"I agree," Father Basko said. "I'm still banking on the big guy."

"The God idea is not possible either," Morgan said. "The man made thing is, I guessed it from researching. I was looking into it before the power went out. Cloud seeding and geoengineering. All that was happening, had happened and something went wrong. I kept saying it."

"To who?" Judd asked. "The Staring people? You said you were alone."

"You know what I mean," she said.

"Do you think Branson will be flooded?" Dawson asked.

Morgan leaned forward. "Is that where you guys are going? Branson?"

Judd nodded.

Father Basko quickly looked at him. "Branson. We were headed there as well when you happened upon us. We heard it on the radio."

"Us ... me, too," Morgan said. "Branson was mentioned on a radio call. Something about a pilgrimage to life."

"No kidding?" Judd said then whistled. "Wow, I didn't know that. We didn't have a radio. We had Ray in Australia, but he disappeared."

Father Basko looked at him curiously. "If you didn't have a radio, how did you choose Branson?"

Judd pointed back to Dawson. "His dream and a brochure."

"Yeah," Dawson said. "I keep dreaming of a guy named Bill. He's waving his arm saying for us to come to Branson."

Morgan laughed. "Oh my God, you were following the dream of a little boy?"

"He was right," Judd said.

"And who is Bill?" Morgan asked. "Some sort of Mother Abagail."

"Actually," Father Basko said. "Bill is the name of the radio man in Branson."

"No kidding." Judd gushed in shock, then looked back at Dawson. "Little dude, you are like a psychic. Next time you dream of Bill pay attention to the surroundings."

"Okay."

"Wow, that is cool. I got chills," Judd held his arm out to Father Basko. "Look goosebumps. Chills."

"Probably the weather," Morgan grumbled.

After giving a scolding look to her via the rearview mirror, Judd focused forward and continued to drive.

They had set a goal of two hundred miles for the day and surpassed that. They had momentum and would had made it father if the weather cooperated and they didn't have to go so far around Columbus. Taking it slow added over an hour to their time. The temperature dropped and the rain was a mixture of water and snow. The cold temperatures caused a deep slush on the road and they pulled over at a small road stop town just across the Indiana border.

Stopping was a must.

They pulled over into the lot of Patty's Bar and Grill. A two story log cabin looking building with a great looking covered patio and fifty yards from a Calico Gas and Go.

"This place looks good." Judd peered close to the windshield. "The chimney is big. Maybe they have a fireplace. Don't see any of those people around either. I'll go check it out. I mean we really have no choice but to stop, Last couple miles were pretty scary on the road."

"I lived in Maine, this is nothing." Father Basko said with a tired voice. "I'm ready to stop though, and the roads ... there will be no street crews to clean this up."

"I know." Judd replied. "Maybe it will warm up. I'll start thinking of something. If it doesn't warm up, roads are gonna be tricky to maneuver."

"I have an idea," Morgan leaned forward. "Why don't we ..."

"Chick," Judd cut her off. "If you suggest one more time that we lose the boat, next leg of the journey you ride in the bus with the creepy kids and Tire Man! Got it?"

She sat back chastised.

Judd grabbed the flashlight and opened the door. "I'll be right back."

The moment he put his foot to the ground he was grateful he was wearing boots. The slushy water hit above his ankles and he could feel how cold it was even through the leather.

He signed with his hand to Sister Helena to wait and he pointed to the building. Judd trudged through the flooded parking lot, up the four steps to the building and opened the door. It didn't smell like bodies which was a good sign. It was cold and dark, the only light came through the large windows and that wasn't much.

It was a big open place with picnic looking tables in the main area. A huge bar was on the far wall, and in the center of the room was a fireplace opened on both sides.

Judd would break the tables if need be for heat.

He heard a splashing sound, and thought maybe it was a leak. Then he realized it was improbable with a second floor above them.

A few steps into his walk he learned the source behind the splashing. It was concealed by the fireplace until Judd moved another few feet.

Against the wall was a huge fish tank, standing before it, back to Judd, was a very large man in a cook's outfit. His hands were in the tank.

"Shit," Judd said out loud.

The man turned around. He had the larger tropical fish dangling from his mouth.

"Sushi on the menu tonight?" Judd joked.

The man chomped and sucked the fish into his mouth, staring at Judd.

"Something tells me, you don't find that funny."

What was taking so long? Dawson wondered. It wasn't like Judd was in the building forever, but sure felt like it. He asked to get out of the car, but that woman kept telling him to stay put. Finally, Father Basko opened the door and Dawson heard it.

A cross between a scream and a sung note, a long drawn out 'Ah' rang out. It grew louder and louder until the front door of Patty's burst open. Some large man wearing white carried Judd face to face by the jacket, feet off the ground as he raged out the door and tossed Judd to the ground. He landed with a splash.

Dawson screamed. The woman in the truck, jumped over the seat and opened the driver's door. Dawson did the same.

Before he even cleared the truck the man in white picked up Judd and tossed him down to the ground again.

"No!" Dawson screamed, his feet sank in the water and he tried to run.

The man in white lowered down to grab Judd once more, but this time, he didn't get too far.

A single gunshot rang out, the Man in White's head jerked up and back and then he fell over.

Dawson didn't think about who shot the Man in White until he ran to Judd. When he wrapped his arms around him was when Dawson saw the new guy.

He stood a little bit away, holding a gun with both hands, like a professional. He lowered it and placed it in a harness he wore over his shoulder and walked to Judd.

His eye and cheek were swollen as if he had been in an accident or something. "You okay?" He offered his hand to Judd.

"Yeah. A little shaken. I'll be fine." Judd took his hand, while still embracing Dawson. He took a moment to peer down to Dawson, reassure him he was fine, then faced the new man again. "Thank you very much."

"You're welcome. It wasn't the way I wanted to make my introduction."

"Doesn't matter. I don't know how you got here, but I sure as hell am glad you arrived," Judd said.

"Good. You may be, but I'm not quite sure how pleased…" the stranger pointed to Morgan, "She will be."

THIRTY-THREE - PLAN

The extra person was going to come in handy. Even though he looked pretty injured, Judd knew Ross was a strong guy and he told them he was a police officer. He told Judd that he saw them somewhere after Columbus and followed them.

There was still a bit of daylight left and a lot to do before settling in for the night. Judd wanted to build a fire for warmth and light. They had to feed everyone, and even though they had food, Judd put Dawson in charge of checking out the kitchen of the restaurant, while he scouted the area.

He went out alone, it was better that way. He left in the middle of a one sided bickering session between Morgan and the new guy, Ross.

Morgan was doing most of the talking.

When he returned, Father Basko, even in his delicate state had gotten a small fire started in the fireplace using what had remained. Ross was moving tables, while Morgan tailed him like a scolding mother. Dawson darted into the dining area, set down a large can of something, then darted out and Sister Helena was wiping down a table while she sipped from a big old glass of what looked like whiskey,

"Indulge much, Sister," Judd said then set the bags of items down on the bar.

"Always enjoyed a sip or two, today calls for more than that." She nodded her head at Morgan.

"Ah," Judd winked. "I get you. Hey Ross, I found batteries for your radio. There are a lot of supplies out there. It's still doing that rain and snow thing but no power, getting gas at the station is gonna be impossible."

"Excellent about the batteries," Ross said. "You know a lot of restaurants have small generators in case the power goes out. Did you look for one here? Maybe we can find one and shut down everything but the pumps. We could run an extension to the station next door so there would be enough power to get some gas."

"Worth a shot," Judd replied. "Good idea."

"Fucking asshole," Morgan quipped.

"Whoa. Whoa," Judd held out his hand to her. "Hey, now. Think you dropped enough F bombs around here to flatten a small city."

"Aren't you cute." Morgan shook her head. "With your witty hick comments."

"What is up your fanny, lady?" Judd asked. "We're all in this together. Okay? Whatever differences you two have you need to put aside."

"Fuck you."

Nervously, Sister Helena approached Morgan. "I don't know why you're so angry, but can you be angry without the swearing, there are children around."

"Really?" Morgan scoffed. "You think swearing is going to affect Dawson? I'm pretty sure he's heard worse on a video game and those … things in the bus can't hear me. Even if they could, they aren't children."

"They're still children," Sister Helena snapped. "That reminds me, Judd, they've been out there long enough. We can't leave them in the cold."

Morgan shook her head in disbelief.

"Maybe it's for the better," Farther Basko suggested. "I mean for safeties sake."

"They are still children," Sister Helena argued.

"What about bringing them in," Ross said. "Put them in one room. Watch them like a hawk."

"How do you think my injuries happened?" Father Basko asked Ross. "I had them in the back room of a building. They did this to me while I slept."

"Jesus," Ross gasped out in shock. "Sorry Sister. Father."

"See." Morgan pointed. "Come on Judd. You have this protective thing about Dawson, you really want to take a chance with those kids around him?"

"I know Dawson doesn't," Judd replied. "They are technically still children. I can't bring myself to do anything to harm them."

"Me either," Ross said.

Morgan huffed. "No shock there. I'm surprised you killed the one today."

"You can say I had a rude awakening," Ross said.

"Look." Morgan peered around to everyone. "I wouldn't bring them in here and I certainly wouldn't let Ross be in charge. For all I know, he'd let them loose on us, steal everything and take off."

"Why would you say that?" Judd asked.

"Because he left me to die. Those things had me and he left me to die. I didn't. My only regret is when he came back for me, they didn't get him."

"Okay. Okay." Judd held up his hand. "Obviously there are issues here. We need to deal with priority things first. Get it warm in here, get gas in our vehicles and get to Branson. From my calculations we are one gas tank away from getting there."

"If you cut lose the boat," Morgan said. "And we don't know if Branson is still viable."

"It's our best hope of something to shoot for," Judd said. "You got a better idea?"

"South," Morgan said. "Go south. This weather is bad. We all know it's going to get worse. South is our best option."

"Branson is south. Not as south as you are talking," Judd said. "If Branson doesn't work out, then I see no reason why we can't go south."

Sister Helena interjected. "We need Branson to get south. I don't know why. It's what Bill said. He's the only gateway. His pilgrimage. That's why he needs to leave in a couple of days. The reason for the hurried evacuation. The two storm systems that are coming are not only causing a mini ice age but dumping enough water to break dams and flood low lying areas so deep ..." she looked at Dawson. "We may need a boat and that's only before it freezes. They've already hit out west, it's only a matter of time and they'll be where we are."

Morgan lowered her head.

Ross pointed at Morgan. "That shut her up. She knows it to be true. She was all over the weather maps."

"How do you know this, Sister?" Morgan asked.

"Bill. I spoke to Bill before the quake," Sister Helena answered. "He received the message and information and was sharing it with everyone who replied."

"Message, like prophetic?" Morgan questioned.

"No." Sister Helena shook her head. "From a weather observation station in Leadville, Colorado. There's life there. One of the areas not hit at all by whatever caused people to drop dead."

Judd's eyes widened and he spun to Sister Helena. "Don't you think you could have shared this info?"

"I thought you knew," she said. "Why else would you be headed west?"

"We didn't get that information either," Ross said. "We couldn't communicate back."

"Life out there is all the more reason not to bring the bus of kids," Morgan said.

"No," Sister Helena shook her head. "They may be able to help the children. Maybe they have a way to bring them back."

"They are brain damaged homicidal time bombs waiting to explode," Morgan said. "They aren't coming back."

Judd whistled. "That's deep. You wanna just leave them behind. Let them freeze and starve?"

"Yes," Father Basko said. "Hating to agree, we can't bring them. We look around this town for another means of transportation and leave them behind. Sister, they're dangerous. We have a healthy child, right here. We can't chance his life. We leave them."

"End it now," Morgan said. "Run a hose from the exhaust into the window of the bus, start the engine, seal the gap and door with duct tape and let them go."

"Holy crap," Judd explained. "Did you just whip that off the top of your head or have you been mentally plotting ways to knock off a bus of kids?"

"You can't kill them," Dawson spoke up emotionally. "Yeah, I think they're bad, but you can't kill them. Judd, tell me you aren't gonna do that?"

"Buddy ..." Judd turned to him. "Do I seem the type?"

Dawson shook his head.

Ross stood and spoke abruptly. "Okay! I'm gonna look for a generator. Dawson, you want to help me?"

Dawson nodded.

Ross placed his hand on Dawson's back and headed toward the kitchen. "Wait until we're out of earshot before you continue the slaughter of the innocent conversation."

Once they were gone from the room, Judd faced Morgan. "I know this is a worry for you and Father.

However, we don't have to make this decision right now. Do we? We have other thigs to do."

Father Basko nodded. "We can discuss it later or tomorrow. But tonight, they can't be in the same room with us."

"I'll scout the upstairs. We'll lock them in a room. No one needs to be near them."

Sister Helena laid her hand on Judd's arm. "I appreciate your kindness, Judd. I cannot look at them and see evil. I see children who need help. I also can't, with a good conscience, leave them behind. If we do, I'll stay with them."

Morgan moved closer. "You would give your life for them? You'd stay behind and die?"

"No one says I would die," Sister Helena replied. "I'll put my fate in God's hands."

"I supposed you have put your fate in God's hands thus far?" Morgan asked.

"I have."

"How's that working out for you?" Morgan snapped. "World's falling apart, freezing over, flooding, people dropped dead, everything is a wasteland. Those things when they turn on you are strong. Big bodies, small bodies, doesn't matter, they are strong. Look what they did to Father Basko. What would they do to Dawson? You for that matter. You're small. Don't take the chance. They'll turn on you. You'll put your life on the line and they will turn on you."

"If it's God's will."

Morgan chuckled. "God's will. Then you're a fucking fool and deserve the fate you get."

Before Judd could comment in shock, Sister Helena was fast. She didn't just slap Morgan, she backhanded her across the face.

Judd immediately intercepted anything that could further happen between the two women.

There was a tense moment of silence in the room, then Morgan turned and walked away. Sister Helena backed up and lifted her drink.

Once Judd knew it was safe he went back to getting things ready for the night, and the next day. Everything was heavy on his mind, the journey, the weather and those children on the bus.

As crass as she was, as hard as Morgan came across, a part of Judd knew she was right. Those kids on the bus were a time bomb and he really hoped Dawson wasn't anywhere near them when the human time bomb went off.

THIRTY-FOUR – FREEZER

Judd watched Morgan sitting off alone, peeling potatoes with more conviction than he had ever seen. Legs slightly parted, elbows on her knees she worked that peeler with a vengeance, she was fast, too.

Nothing had been said to her all evening, she grabbed her dinner and walked off by herself. Things had quieted down. Both Father Basko and Dawson were asleep in the camp they made around the fireplace. Sister Helena was dozing on and off. Judd believed she was three sheets to the wind. She hit the bottle pretty hard, especially since it had been difficult to corral the twelve kids and Tire Man from the bus to an upstairs room. Twelve kids no younger than Dawson, but no older than about eleven. They wouldn't budge from the bus at first, but when Judd pulled out the prepackaged peanut butter and jelly sandwich, they all followed. That one sandwich was used to lure them up to the steps and into the room.

It was funny and scary the way they all dove for it when he threw it inside. He and Ross put them in a small room, the only one they could lock and Judd could hear the footsteps on the ceiling. They were contained, that was good.

Ross made a joke that it sounded like a, "Party in the upstairs apartment."

It was a great analogy. Judd knew before long, the "party sounds" would be buried beneath the storm that was brewing. The thunder that roared in the distance during dinner, increasingly grew louder and stronger.

Judd was hyper. He had accomplished a lot with Ross, getting gas and supplies for the next day. He wanted to play his guitar, it always calmed him, but he didn't want to wake

Father Basko. He knew it wouldn't wake Dawson, he was a heavy sleeper. After watching Morgan work those potatoes, he finally walked over to her. It was time to break the ice, to maybe try to smooth things out.

Judd cleared his throat. "That's some impressive peeling. You working out frustration."

"No." She looked up. "I'm peeling potatoes."

"What for?"

"I don't plan on sleeping tonight. Not with Village of the Damned above our heads. So I'm gonna put these in the pot on the fire and we'll have them for breakfast before we hit the road. The hot dogs were good. We just need substance."

With a closed mouth, Judd nodded and sat down.

Morgan paused in her peeling and looked at him intensely.

"What? I can't join you?"

She huffed and shook her head. "Suit yourself."

"You know … When I was …"

"Stop," she said. "You are gonna try to tell me some stupid story."

"You don't want to hear it?"

"No." She shook her head and peeled. "Spare me."

"So says the girl who got beat up by a nun."

She glared at him.

"Don't let it get you down. You're in good company. Many of Catholic school kids back in the day had a run in or two with a wayward ruler and a wicked sister."

"You aren't funny."

"Yeah, I am." Judd nudged her.

"Really? You just touched me."

"Oh, stop. What is up with you? Why are you so nasty?"

"You really want to know?" she asked.

"I do."

"I'm angry. I am really angry and I can't shake it."

"About the kids?"

"No, that worries me. It really does. I saw how they can be. They attacked once, they'll attack again. That's not why I'm angry. I'm not a bad person, I'm not. I was always the unselfish one. A lot of good that did me. I'm mad because I didn't resolve my life. The world dropped dead when I was screaming at the only man I ever loved. Despite the fact ..." she tossed a potato and grabbed another. "That he cheated on me and left me, I still loved him. I'm pissed it never got resolved. I'm mad because the last words I said to him I'm pretty sure weren't very nice."

"Yeah, I'm pretty sure of that, too."

She shook her head. "Ross tells me to forgive him. I want to forgive him, but I am so mad because he died and I didn't." She paused. "It sounds stupid but I can't shake it, and it comes out in everything I do and say. Eventually I'll stop, if you know ... someone else doesn't leave me to die."

"Well, I'm sure he had his reasons."

Morgan chuckled in disbelief. "Did you really just say that?"

"I did. And I can promise I won't leave you to die."

"I believe that."

"If it makes you feel better you're not alone with those feelings. When this thing happened, I was at a construction site, standing on the ninth floor of an unfinished building with my best friend. He was joking about falling over, I was too and then he did."

"I'm sorry."

"Me, too."

"Is that what you did?" she asked. "Construction?"

"Actually, no, I was a country music star."

Morgan laughed. "I never heard of Judd Heston, but hey, thanks for the laugh."

"On that note, you're no longer as nasty, I've accomplished something this evening. I'll let you get back to your potatoes."

"Thanks."

Judd stood.

"And Judd, really, thanks."

Judd tipped his head and made his way over to the only other person awake. Ross. Ross was on the floor with a toolbox next to him. He was unscrewing legs from chairs and tables for the fire. Judd sat down a few feet from Dawson and joined Ross.

"So," Judd asked. "Did you really leave her to die?"

Ross stared at him for a moment. "Yeah, I did. That's not me. She was bitching at me when they attacked and I just bolted."

Judd looked over his shoulder at Morgan. "Yeah, I can see where that can happen."

Ross laughed. "I changed my mind. She let me have it." He pointed to his face. "I deserved it."

"It works for you."

"Can I ask you something? This is gonna sound off. Maybe it's just a coincidence that you have that guitar and you look like him, but are you Judd Bryant?"

Judd smiled. "I am."

"Oh, man, me and my kids loved 'Carrot Cake and Karen'. We'd dance to it all the time. Man ... I am a huge fan."

"Thank you. That means a lot."

"So is Heston your real name?" Ross asked. "I know Dawson called you Mr. Heston one or two times."

"Now that ..." Judd waved his finger. "Is a long story for another time."

Both of them looked up when a loud 'crack' of lightening shook the ground and lit up the room.

"Holy shit!" Judd exclaimed.

Within seconds, the rain blasted at the window and the wind was so strong, the flame on the fire flickered.

"Do you hear that?" Morgan asked, standing.

It's the storm." Judd said.

"No." she shook her head.

THUMP.

"That."

"I'm sure it's nothing," Judd replied. "Probably a tree or something hitting against us."

Thump.

Ross pointed. "It woke the boy."

Dawson rubbed his eyes and walked over to Judd.

"What's the matter, buddy?" Judd asked. "You can't sleep? The storm wake you?"

"Bill did," Dawson said groggy.

"What do you mean? A dream?"

Thump.

"Judd," Morgan called him. "Something is up."

Again, a loud crack and clap shook the building.

"It's the storm." Judd looked down to Dawson. "So you dreamt of Bill?"

"Yes." Dawson nodded.

Thump. Thump.

Ross slowly stood and peered to the ceiling. "She's right. It's not the storm."

"I'm scared," Dawson held on to Judd.

"It's okay." Judd embraced. "It was just a dream. What did Bill say?"

The thumping grew louder and faster. Judd stood up, releasing his hold on Dawson.

"He said ... run."

Judd's eyes widened.

Ross pointed. "The staircase."

"Stay here," Judd ordered and walked to the corner of the restaurant with Ross and Morgan.

"Judd, no!" Dawson cried.

"Stay over there." Judd held out his hand.

Dawson listened. He stayed by the fire while Judd, Ross and Morgan stared at the door.

"It's quiet," Ross said. "I thought they were in the stairwell."

"Me, too," Judd said.

Morgan shook her head. "They are. You can't hear them with the storm."

Judd whispered and pointed to the door. "Did we lock this?"

Ross shook his head. "I don't think we did."

"Shit," Judd said. "It locks from the other side." He slowly reached for the knob.

Morgan stopped him. 'What are you doing?"

"If they aren't in the stairwell, I'm locking it." Again, his hand reached and again he was stopped.

Ross moved him aside. "Let me. Okay?" He pulled his weapon. "Stay back."

Judd and Morgan stepped back.

Ross extended his hand.

"This is silly," Judd said. "There's nothing ..."

With a thunderous 'crash' the door flew entirely from the hinges, slamming into Ross and sending his gun sliding across the linoleum as he hit the floor.

Tire Man charged out and behind him raced the twelve kids.

Judd's first thought was Dawson, and as he turned, Tire Man face palmed him so hard it sent him back crashing into a table.

Morgan ran.

She made it only a few feet, when one of the Bus kids dove on her back. She tried to shuck the child, but his arm gripped around her neck, strangling her. Her only defense was the potato peeler and she jammed it in the child's arm. He released her and she flew over by Dawson.

She arrived in time to intercept another bus kid who came for him. Lifting Dawson into her arms, she pushed the child away with her foot and ran toward the door.

"Judd!" Dawson screamed. "Judd."

Get Dawson to safety. Get him out. Was all she could think of. The truck was the best option. She opened the front door and quickly realized that wasn't the answer. A gust of wind acted like a wall she was unable to push through, it sent her back a foot just as a huge piece of debris flew at the door and bounced off. Then in a split second, the wind pulled back, sucking her through. One arm holding Dawson, reaching for the door, Morgan struggled with her footing. Finally her fingers touched the door. She turned her body to close it when a bus kid leapt at her.

She was fast, darting out of the way, the bus kid sailed through the archway and she slammed the door.

She was far from being safe inside the restaurant. It was mayhem and Morgan was so focused on getting Dawson to safety, she tried not to see all that was going on. Dawson was heavy, and it took a lot to hold on to him, especially when he fought and screamed for Judd.

In her mad dash across the dining room floor of the restaurant, she spotted Sister Helena. One bus kid was on her back, while another flailed her fists relentlessly at her.

In her run by Sister Helena, Morgan grabbed hold of the hair of the fist-throwing little brat, yanked her back to the floor and grabbed Sister Helena's hand, pulling her with her.

In the kitchen, she raced to the walk in freezer, opened it and put Dawson in side. "Stay here. You'll be safe."

She pushed the door closed and turned to help Sister Helena.

The nun was on the floor with the boy on her back. Morgan grabbed the first thing she could, a small pot, and she hit the child with it. When he paused, she used her foot to kick him from Sister Helena, grabbed her hand, dragged her to her feet and pushed her into the freezer.

"Stay with Dawson!" Morgan yelled. "The door opens from inside. Do not open until you hear silence."

She didn't stay long, the last vision of them was Dawson running to the door and Sister Helena reaching for him. She slammed the door shut.

They were safe.

Of that she was sure.

No sooner did she turn around, then bus kid ran at her. Morgan charged back, grabbing him in her momentum and carrying him through the swinging kitchen door.

Father Basko.

Ross didn't understand, maybe it was an advantage, but when he stood from being knocked down, the rabid children never attacked him. They were too busy pursuing Sister Helena and even more so, Father Basko. Seven of them pounced the priest. While Judd engaged in a cat and mouse game with Tire Man. Only Judd was the mouse.

Ross didn't know where to go first, who to help.

He picked his battle and aimed for Father Basko.

The attacking bus kids were like pit bulls. They pounced, grabbed, pulled and kicked, and each one he tossed off, merely jumped back and returned.

He was so focused on getting the kids off Father Basko, he didn't realize it was too late.

His feet slipped and he slid in a pool of blood that came from the priest. Ross didn't want to look, he didn't want to see what they had done. In the midst of his battle, he saw it. The fire extinguisher hanging by the stairwell. He ran to it, grabbed it and raced back over to those kids attacking Father Basko.

He blasted it and the white substance stunned them. They paused in their attack, rubbed their faces and moved in confused circles.

After dropping the extinguisher, Ross grabbed two of them. He was strong enough to carry them both and he took them to the stairwell, tossed them hard inside, and ran back for two more before the ones in the stairwell could catch their bearings.

He put them in and reached down for the door. Just as he grabbed it, he saw Morgan.

"Here. In here." Ross yelled.

She raced over with the kid, and using the weight of her body, along with her arms, she flung the boy inside with the others. Ross slammed the door against the jam. It didn't take long for the door to move from the weight of the kids trying to get out.

"Think you can hold this?" Ross asked.

"I will," Morgan replied. She pressed her back against the door and locked her legs.

Ross stepped away. He looked for Judd. He was behind the bar, sailing bottles at Tire Man. It distracted Ross enough that he didn't see the little girl coming, she jumped up at him, fingers digging into his neck.

Holding her to him, bracing her by the scruff of her neck, Ross raged for the front door of the bar, grabbing another child in his run.

The door opened easily with the force of the wind and Ross hoisted one child out, then grabbed the girl, yanking her from him tossing her out as well.

He shut and locked the door.

It was less chaotic and Ross lost count of how many kids from the bus there were.

It was under control, at least with the kids. There were three standing calmly in the middle of the restaurant, staring out. One of them had a potato peeler in his arm.

After catching his breath, Ross grabbed a chair, carried it over to the bar. "Enough of this shit." He lifted it high and smashed Tire Man over the head.

He toppled to the ground. Ross hit him again just to be sure he was down.

Judd stood up.

"You okay?" Ross asked.

"I couldn't get by him," Judd said. "He was kicking my ass."

"Join the club."

"Dawson?" Judd asked in a panic.

"He's fine," Morgan answered. "He's in the freezer with Sister Helena. Can you guys …" her body bounced. "Help?"

Ross walked over to the fireplace and grabbed the tool box. He lifted a couple chair legs and carried them to the stairwell. "Sorry." He said to Morgan. "Just hold it another minute." He grabbed a hammer and nails, placed the nails in his mouth, then lifted a leg to the arch and began securing the door.

"How many are in there?" Judd asked.

"Five," Ross answered as he hammered. "I tossed two out."

"Three," Morgan corrected. "I threw one out as well." She stepped away from the door, turned and held it with her hands for Ross.

"One is missing" Judd said.

"We'll find it." Morgan secured the next leg to the door. He only needed a couple nails, enough for a temporary fix.

"Oh my God, Father Basko," Judd said.

"I know." Ross paused in his hammering, looking over his shoulder. Judd was standing by Father Basko's body, or rather what remained of it. He paused then finished the final nail. "We'll take care of …" he turned around and caught his breath. "take care of …" His eyes widened.

"What?" Morgan asked, then turned around.

Tire Man was standing, dead eye stare locked on Judd and he held Ross' gun haphazardly in his hand.

"Judd!" Morgan screamed, "Watch out."

Judd spun around.

Ross saw Judd dart out of the way, and Ross ran, hammer in hand, toward Tire Man.

The gun went off, a split second before Ross, two hands on the handle of the hammer, like a baseball player, swung upwards with everything he had, landing the hammer claw end first in the base of Tire Man's skull. Tire Man teetered and the gun dropped from his hand. Quickly, Ross swept up the gun, shifted his body and fired once at Tire Man, hitting him in the side of the neck and taking him down once and for all.

Ross' heart raced out of control. He bent over, hands to his legs to catch his breath. It was close. Especially when he saw Tire Man with the gun. He was confident, especially with the way Tire Man held the gun, that everything was okay.

He knew he was wrong when he heard the sound of Morgan's voice like he never heard it before.

Soft, sad and whimpering, "Ross."

He held his eyes closed tight for a moment and slowly lifted his head and looked.

Morgan knelt on the floor. Blood flowed over her fingers as she tried with diligence to stop the bleeding with her bare hands.

Judd had been shot.

THIRTY-FIVE – RATTLED

"Get me this, get me that, find me this, find me that." Ross was a plethora of orders and Morgan followed them as fast and best as she could.

Each item, he asked for, she found. Either he had it, or Sister Helena did in her bag.

He was on the floor working diligently on Judd. There wasn't time to worry about the remaining kids, they could only hope they remained calm while he tried to stabilize Judd.

"Just make sure you keep the Sister and Dawson away. At least until I'm done," Ross said. "We don't need either of them seeing this."

"Should I tell them something?"

Ross looked at her, his eyes cased her bloody shirt. "Not until you change."

Morgan understood.

"Hey," Judd said groggily. "What's all the fuss about?"

"He's awake," Ross said. "Hand me the whiskey."

"It's a good sign, right?" Morgan asked.

Ross didn't reply to her, he took the bottle and lifted Judd's head. "I need you to take a big drink. I mean huge, okay."

"Why?"

"You've been shot, Pal."

It was long and dragged out as Judd said the word in surprise. "What? No way."

"Yeah, way."

"It can't be bad."

Ross tilted his head. "It's bad."

"But you're a cop and if you're fixing me then I'm good. It can't be that bad."

"You don't have a choice," Ross said. "Plus, you're in luck. I was a medic in the reserves."

"Sweet. So how bad is bad?"

"Bad. You lost a shit load of blood."

"Eh, I'll get it back."

Ross exhaled in frustration. "I need you to be quiet and still. Morgan, keep the light close."

"Ah, you two are talking again," Judd said.

"Judd, please. Morgan, the vodka."

"I just had whiskey."

"It's not for drinking." Ross took the uncapped bottle from Morgan. "This is going to hurt." He poured it over the wound left of his naval.

"Ow."

Ross smiled. "That was simple. I think I see it. You need to hold still, I think I can get it. Hold the light closer Morgan."

Judd grunted an "Uh!" loudly.

Ross looked at him. "I didn't touch you."

"You're gonna reach in me with your fingers?" Judd asked, "That's how President Harrison died."

"What?"

"They reached in with their fingers and he got an infection and died."

"Well, there was a bag with rubber gloves and antibiotics," Ross said.

"Hey, that was me. I got them." Judd replied.

"Good for you and by the way, it was Garfield, not Harrison."

"You sure?"

"Positive. Now hold still," Ross instructed and reached into the wound.

The screams carried to them, even through the insulated metal door of the freezer. A long cry out, then another, and then silence.

Dawson scurried to the door and Sister Helena held him back.

"That was Judd," Dawson cried out. "I know it was. He's hurt. Judd doesn't scream."

"You can't leave here."

"Let me go help Judd."

"Dawson!" Sister Helena scolded. "No. More than anything Judd wants you safe. Honor him, stay put."

Dawson nodded sadly, then placed his arms around Sister Helena's waist. When he did he saw the blood and stepped back. "You're hurt." He looked at her arms, deep gashes ran up and down them.

"I'll be fine." She brought him back into the fold of her embrace. "So will Judd."

Judd had passed out. He cried out in pain a few times and then his head dropped to the side and he was out. Even though Ross was happy that he was talking, he needed him still and silent.

He was able to pull the shell from his gut but Ross hadn't a clue how much damage was done. He did his best to seal the wound using everything from a needle and thread to duct tape. After he had finished, they carried him to a sleeping bag near the fire.

"What do you think?" Morgan asked.

Ross shook his head. 'Your guess is as good as mine. He lost a lot of blood."

"He said we're close to Branson. Can we go?"

"You mean like now?" Ross asked.

Morgan nodded. "Yeah, what if we go right now? We'll be there by morning."

"You hear that out there?" Ross shook his head. "I don't know."

"We have to try. They may have a doctor there."

"I know. Let's hit the radio again. He has extra batteries. We can keep trying. Once the storm breaks, we'll head out even if it's not light."

"It's not going to break, Ross. You know that."

Ross closed his eyes,

"What about them?" Morgan nodded her head at the three children. "We can't trust them around him."

"Once we get Dawson and Sister Helena from the freezer, we'll put them in there." Ross then groaned. "Oh man, Dawson. He is not going to handle this well. We're going to ..." Slowly, Ross lifted his eyes upward. "Oh. No." He stood.

"What's wrong?" Morgan asked.

Ross heard it, didn't she?

"What's wrong?" Morgan asked.

"Do you hear that?"

"I don't hear anything."

"Exactly." Ross raced to the door.

"It's over, we can go. It stopped."

Ross knew better, he opened the door. The air was still and not a single rain drop fell.

"Let's get everybody," Morgan joined him. "We'll carry him out."

"No." Focused Ross stepped out and on to the porch,

"Where are the kids we threw out?"

Ross didn't answer that question. The night was suddenly quiet. It was filled with an eerie silence and a greenish hue as if the moon was shining through a color gel.

He stepped down the stairs and to the lot, the moment he did he felt the first 'pat' to this head, then suddenly it fell around him. He held out his hand to catch the hail that was the size of peanuts. He shifted his eyes around when the pressure filled his ears, then heard the roar. Almost like a freight train in the distance,

He spun back to Morgan. "Get inside."

"What's going on."

Where was it? He looked around. Where? The sky was dark until it lit up with six or seven bolts of lightning that speared through the sky continuously, brightening it.

That was when he saw the first funnel in the distance straight ahead of him, it was huge, as he turned to run back in the house, he saw the second one, it filled the entire sky.

"Oh my God," Morgan gasped out in shock. "The basement?"

"There is no basement." Ross moved toward Morgan to get her inside.

"What are we going to do?" Morgan ran inside, then stopped. "The Freezer."

"Grab Judd."

Quickly, each of them grabbed an end of the sleeping bag, using it like a stretcher to carry Judd.

"How long?" Morgan asked.

"I don't know. A minute."

"That one is headed straight toward us."

"They don't move in a straight line. It may veer off, we're still getting caught in the wind."

When they arrived in the kitchen, the one bus kid lay on the floor by the freezer door. His forehead was bloody and there were bloody handprints on the freezer. It was obvious he ran over and over to into the door until he knocked himself unconscious.

"Sister!" Ross yelled. "Open the door."

"She can't hear us."

Ross tried again. "Open the door!"

The freezer door opened and Sister Helena gasped. "Oh my Sweet Lord."

"Judd!" Dawson screamed.

Hurriedly they carried him inside and set him down. Ross ran back to the door.

"Where are you going?" Morgan asked.

"We can't lose everything. Stay here." Ross closed the door and ran as fast as he could back to the dining room.

The windows rattled and the noise of the impending tornados was deafening. He grabbed two backpacks in his run, tossing them over his shoulder, then the case with the radio.

His heart pounded and he couldn't think straight. Where were the batteries? The room had been thrown into disarray from the chaotic run in. Finally he saw the bag by the fireplace, he lifted that and a duffle bag that was on the floor.

The funnel was close, he could feel the ground vibrating. He headed back to the kitchen, arms full but stopped, there was one more thing. Even though he didn't have time to spare, Ross ran back to the dining area and grabbed it ... Judd's guitar.

He balanced everything in his arms as he rushed back to the kitchen. His call for them to open the door was buried in the wind noise. He dropped the bags and opened the freezer. He shoved the items in with his foot then ran in just as a loud crack and boom rang out.

He dropped the items, slammed the door, and held it closed while catching his breath.

There was a certain amount of sound proofing in the freezer, but he could still hear things clamoring and banging outside.

Inside though was a solo sobbing sound.

Dawson.

He didn't want to let go of the door, so Ross looked over his shoulder.

Dawson was seated on his knees. He held on to Judd's hand and lifted his tear filled eyes to Ross. "Please tell me he's going to be okay. Please. Don't let him die. Please."

Ross didn't know what to say. More than anything he wanted to tell the child it was going to be alright, but he couldn't. All Ross could do was turn away, face the silver of the door and hold on as best as he could.

THIRTY-SIX – FORTUNE AND FAME

"Branson, anyone, anyone out there? Do you read?" Morgan called out. "Anyone? Over." She switched the channel.

Ross reached over and stopped her. "Give it a few minutes before switching."

Morgan nodded.

Sister Helena called from the backseat. "Can we go any faster?"

"No, Sister," Ross answered. "Water on the road is deep. I don't want to stall." He turned the defrosters on to clear the windshield, but it wasn't helping. A steady thin rain mixed with snow fell and Ross prayed the water didn't freeze. They were headed south, it had to get warmer.

Go faster, Ross thought. They were so lucky they were even on the road at all.

He thought back to the moment they opened the freezer door. Things had quieted down and they had been in there safely for over an hour.

Judd regained consciousness pretty fast and was a great patient. He took the pain pills and the antibiotics and even joked about how bad his luck was.

His demeanor was a good sign. It didn't help the horrified feeling Ross had before he looked beyond the confines of the walk in freezer.

He had no idea what waited beyond the door. It was time to find out.

A simple creak of the door brought in a blast of cooler air and a fine mist of water. He could hear the dripping and expected the worst.

Tornados were peculiar things. Ross remembered the time as a kid when he lived in Kentucky, His grandmother's house was spared during a tornado and the next door neighbor's home was flattened.

It was dark when he stepped inside the kitchen, but he could see enough with the help of a flashlight that things had been toppled. He had the others stay behind while he checked it out. He looked up, part of the ceiling was missing. It was a two story building, he was pretty sure the top floor was gone.

A light rain carried in as he walked into the main dining area. His primary goal was to go outside, canvas a way to get out of town, if there was indeed a way. They needed to get to Branson, it was their only hope for help.

The restaurant for the most part was intact. Windows were busted and the door was off the hinges. The area above the bar had collapsed and most of the upper floor was in the dining area.

The place where Father Basko had died was buried.

Ross made his way outside. It was black, he could barely see anything outside his flashlight beam. He moved it left to right. The school bus was on its side and against the buildings across the road. The convenience store was flattened, however before him was nothing short of a miracle.

Even though it was covered with debris, Judd's truck, complete with the boat, was essentially unharmed and still parked right where they had left it.

Ross had seen instances like it before, though rare, it wasn't impossible. He was forever grateful. He would see better once the sun emerged, but until then, Ross worked on clearing the debris from the truck.

It started, had gas, and just before five in the morning, they carried Judd to the truck and were on the road. Slowly, but moving.

Daylight brought the clarity that the entire area had been devastated.

Chunks of woods, papers and even bodies floated in the shallow flooding that covered the area, causing Ross to drive with caution.

Morgan sat up front attacking the radio.

Judd lay on the back seat, his head on Sister Helena's lap, while Dawson sat on the floor behind Morgan's seat, his hand continuously on Judd.

Judd waned between being awake and asleep, he even tried to talk and joke. Ross knew he wasn't well. His color was horrible, a pasty white, but Ross wasn't giving up hope. Judd was a strong man, fighting with everything he had both physically and emotionally.

Ross was determined to get Judd the help he needed. It was out there, and Ross pressed forward at a safe speed. That was all he could do.

A 'thud' against the bottom of the truck stirred Judd from his sleep. When he opened his eyes it was daylight, the last time he woke up it was still dark.

"What the heck are you hitting?" he asked.

"Lots of things in the road," Ross answered. "How are you feeling?"

"Sore." That wasn't completely the truth, his entire body felt aflame with pain and he had the bed spins when he closed his eyes. "I keep dreaming of Morgan calling out 'anyone'."

Morgan looked over her shoulder. "I'm going to get someone on this damn thing."

"Well how dee damn, you are in a good mood and no fighting. Guess my accident isn't a bad thing after all."

"Rest," Sister Helena swiped her hand across his brow. "Please."

"Nah, I'm good Sister. But you can keep touching my forehead. It reminds me of my mom." Judd could feel Dawson, but he couldn't see him. He tried, but he was at his feet and Judd couldn't lift his head enough to see him. "Hey little buddy, how you doing?"

"Sad," Dawson said. "I'm scared, Judd. Scared for you. You look like a zombie."

"Dawson," Sister Helena scolded calmly.

"No, kidding? Really?" Judd asked. "How cool. I was never very vain. I feel good."

"You look bad," Dawson said, "You gotta get better Judd. You found me, you have to stay with me."

"Buddy, I am going to give it my all." Judd cringed in pain. It hurt to talk, to breathe. "I could use one of those pain pills right about now, and that bottle I watched you pick up from the rubble."

"Judd," Sister Helena said softly. "You shouldn't mix pills and alcohol."

"He can have them," Ross said. "I think it will be fine."

Morgan handed back the bottle and pills as Sister Helena lifted his head so he could take them. Judd coughed when the pill lodged for a second in his throat. He washed it down with more booze.

"You know what's funny?" Judd asked. "If I was shot before all this happened, man my music would outlive me."

"Not that you're going anywhere," Ross said. "Your music is gonna outlive you anyhow."

"He saved your guitar." Dawson said.

"No kidding?" Judd said, "That's really swell. Hopefully I'll play it again. I want Dawson to know my music."

"I know your music." Ross said. "Every word." He then began to sing, "*Walking in the rain, feeling no more pain, Jack and Jim my best friend again. I can stumble, I can fall, I can take it all, but the addictions in my blood ...keeps me heart a flarin'...*"

At that instant, everyone but Judd sang, "Craven Carrot Cake and Karen."

Judd laughed and coughed. "You all know it."

Morgan looked to the back seat with a bright smile. "That was you? Oh my God, I love that song. You're famous."

"Was."

"Is," Dawson corrected, "Everyone knows who Mr. Heston is."

Before anything else was said, a hiss of static captured everyone's attention.

"This is Branson, responding to unknown caller. Anyone there?"

As if they won some sort of championship, everyone in the truck cheered.

Morgan grabbed the radio. "We're here. We hear you." She looked behind her to Judd. "We need help."

THIRTY-SEVEN – LAST CHORD

They were filled with hope. Even though the slow moving trip was taking longer than it should have, they were in contact with Branson.

"Radio when you're within fifty miles. You may run into trouble. We'll look for you," Bill from Branson told them.

Ross didn't know what that meant, maybe they had trucks out on the roads. As instructed they checked in every fifty miles. Sometimes with a longer reply, most with a "Roger that."

They put the last of the gas in the tank, with a little over a hundred miles to go. Only in a few places did the water ever recede.

Two hundred miles before Branson, Judd started to cough. He talked less, and slept more. Sister Helena said he was burning up.

Fifty miles before Branson, they placed their final radio call and they didn't think too much of the lack of response, until only three miles later, the journey ended.

The road just ended and nothing but a huge lake of water blocked their way. The water washed back and forth in a wave like manner against the concrete, almost as if it was always there, a natural lake.

Tips of trees poked through the dark water, but there was nothing more as far as the eye could see.

Ross stepped from the truck. He knew the temperature had dropped, but he didn't realize how cold it was.

Too cold to rain, that was for sure, even though the sky was clouded over. Ross spread the map out on the hood of the truck. "Branson is by that mountain range." He exhaled in frustration. "What now?"

"You know, from the moment Judd picked me up, I bitched about cutting the boat loose." She tilted her head in a nod to the boat. "I've never been so happy to be wrong."

"Do you know anything about boats?"

"Nope. Do you?"

"Not enough. Should we stay here?"

"No, we have to try. We'll layer up clothing, we have to try."

"He's sick, Morgan. If it rains, the cold ..."

"We have to try. Those aren't rain clouds. They're too high. This ..." She pointed up. "Is snow. We need to move."

He was hesitant, but eventually he agreed.

It was the trickiest thing he had ever done in his life and it reiterated to Ross how much he didn't know. It was all guess work.

Judd helped. He woke enough to explain how to unhitch the boat and coughed his way through explaining how to get the motor going and how to steer, explaining it was like a lawn mower.

He loaded Judd, Dawson and the supplies in the boat first. Once he had the boat near the water's edge, Sister Helena got in, and Ross and Morgan pushed the boat out, climbing in once they cleared the road.

It was so cold it hurt and the muscles in his legs cramped.

A chill set into his bones and he knew it wasn't going away anytime soon. The cold wind that continuously blew didn't help either. He hated starting the motor and the speed of the boat made it even colder. So many bodies floated in water, they looked like logs.

Morgan kept trying the radio.

Nothing.

It was a mistake, a huge mistake getting in the boat. Ross felt it, he knew for certain when the water thickened with sludge and ice and the motor fluttered and finally stalled.

The boat stopped moving. Ross tried and tried again to start it, however it was useless.

They were going nowhere.

Surrounded by gray chunks of concrete and ice that floated by. Unfortunately, they were at a standstill.

In the quiet of nature's newest Missouri lake, Ross resolved they had reached the end of their journey.

He felt horrible for Dawson. The little boy was covered in a blanket, never leaving Judd's side. Every time Judd's body shook with a cough, Dawson hugged him.

"I'm sorry," Morgan said. "We should have stayed."

"No." Ross shook his head. "What's meant to be was meant to be. I just... I just can't figure out why we made it this far. What was the point?"

"Maybe it's bigger than us," Sister Helena said. "Perhaps there was a reason beyond our knowledge that we were meant to be. Maybe being something to each other before we leave this earth was enough."

Immediately, Ross looked at Morgan.

"What?" she asked.

"Usually, you make an anti-God statement at this time."

"Nah, not this time." She glanced at Dawson. "There are no atheists in this foxhole right now."

"Oh my God, people," Judd spoke weakly. "You all are so morbid. I'm the one that's dying here."

"Judd no," Dawson whimpered. "Please don't say that."

"Sorry, Buddy." Judd tried to sit up. "You guys are moping."

Whispering, Ross leaned to him. "We're stalled. We're stuck. It's cold. We aren't going anywhere. We're at the end of the line."

"For now. There's a reason," Judd said.

"What would that be?" Ross asked.

"My legacy. My song. I have to make sure it lives on."

"I know it." Ross laughed.

"Yeah, but do you know the chords?" Judd asked, then coughed. "Sister, I know you have a journal. Was it saved?'

"I ... I think." She grabbed her backpack. "Yes. Yes it was."

"Grab a pen, write down these chords. Ross needs them. Morgan, can you hand me my guitar?"

"Sure." Morgan grabbed it.

Judd tried to inch his way to a sitting position. He grunted and Ross helped him up. He then placed the strap over Judd's head.

Weakly, he placed his hand on the guitar. He eyes rolled slightly and his head jerked as he caught himself dozing off. He muttered the simple three chord progression of the verse, then the chorus to Sister Helena, then struck an off tune chord.

"You gonna play, Judd?" Dawson asked.

"I am. Not very good. Not very fast, but I need to play. Join in if you know it."

The beat wasn't as fast as the recording, and in the stand still boat, Judd struggled to play.

Steam emerging from their mouths, they slowly sang with Judd. Their voices echoing across the water filled land.

"Walking in the rain, feeling no more pain, Jack and Jim my best friends again. I can stumble, I can fall, I can take it all, but the addictions in my blood ...keeps me heart a flarin'..."

"Craving ..." Judd sang, then stopped. His head tilted back.

"Judd? Judd!" Dawson screamed out panicked.

"Look." Judd peered up to the sky. "An angel."

Ross felt heartbroken when Judd said that, until he heard the distant flutter of a helicopter. "Judd. That's not an angel. It's a chopper. We're saved. We're saved."

Silence.

Ross' eyes met Dawson's as the little boy clutched Judd's hand and his head fell to Judd's chest.

The glory and excitement of the hovering rescue was shrouded in a gloom, far darker than the clouds.

Judd ... was gone.

THIRTY-EIGHT – BRANSON

Branson, Missouri was gone. Technically it was still there, but under water. Those who survived the drop of humanity, heard about the storms and retreated to the Branson Airport twelve hundred feet above sea level.

Bill Thomas ran the airport and greeted them when they arrived.

He was just like Dawson dreamt. A little older, a little thicker, but he looked and sounded the same as he had in his dreams.

"Out west there's not much, but there's life and civilization," Bill said. "We have enough fuel for one more flight out."

Dawson didn't hear much about where they were going. Somewhere in Colorado. He heard Bill explain to Ross that it was some sort of manmade incident gone bad. That's what they were thinking, and nature took over.

They believed the water was going to keep on rising for a while so they were headed to high elevation areas.

"It will end up becoming a whole new geographical world," Bill told them.

Dawson didn't know what that meant. He half listened. He was more concerned about Judd. He didn't want to leave him, he couldn't leave him.

"I'm sorry, little man, I really am." Ross said. "We're going to get cleaned up and get some new clothes. You wanna come, or stay here?"

"I want to stay with Judd for a little bit."

"Okay you do that. Listen," Ross crouched down. "You're not alone. You have us, alright. We're here for you."

Dawson nodded.

"Will he be okay?" Morgan asked.

"I'm here," Sister Helena said. "I'll stay. Go get fresh clothes."

Dawson sat on the floor by Judd's covered body. At least they didn't leave him behind.

The chopper could have left Judd, but the pilot didn't.

They airlifted them all, one by one, including Judd into the chopper.

Because of the radio calls, they knew there was an injured man, and a paramedic was on board. He tried with diligence to revive Judd the entire short flight to Branson, but it was futile.

Dawson wanted to cry, he just couldn't believe his friend was gone. He was in shock. He kept waiting for Judd to open his eyes. He never did. He died with the guitar in his hands.

The adults around him talked about a reason for this and a reason for that. Dawson wanted and needed a reason why Judd left him. However, nobody could give him one.

Judd made a promise and kept it.

He kept Dawson safe all the way to Branson.

That meant something to Dawson. He knew his parents would be happy about that. All those people Dawson knew were now gone, those he loved ... gone. It was now his job, his responsibility to keep them alive, to honor them. His parents ... and Judd.

Even at his young age, he knew the best way to do that was to live and survive.

It would be a different way of life, but he would give it his best shot.

He didn't really have a choice. His parents and Judd would have wanted that.

EPILOGUE – SEVEN YEARS LATER

His knuckles made a popping noise when he clenched his cramping fingers into a fist. "Damn it," Dawson shook his hand.

"Language." Came the voice in another room.

"He heard that?" Dawson shook his head. "Man."

He lay on his single bed in a bedroom he shared in the three room apartment in Leadville Nine. It was small, but it was home. Everything was neat and tidy, always, except his corner of the room.

Note book sprawled out next to him, Dawson lifted a pencil, wrote a sentence, bobbed his head, hummed a little, then stuck the pencil in his mouth before working out the chord progression on the guitar.

He had it. He almost had it when there was a knock on his door.

"Aw, man."

It opened and Ross stepped in. "Hey, now, let's go. You know Joe only comes to do hair once a month. You miss this appointment I'm cutting your hair myself."

Dawson groaned. The last time Ross cut his hair it was horrible. He was twelve and Ross made so many mistakes Dawson ended up nearly bald.

Dawson used to say he got stuck with Ross. When they arrived in Leadville after the events, it was supposed to be temporary, but they never left.

Ross immediately 'claimed' him, telling Dawson, "I had children, I can do this. Okay?"

"Yeah okay." Dawson was eight. He figured that was what he had to do.

Ross wasn't a bad guy, he was tough and strict yet Dawson was really glad he had him.

Ross immediately was given a job in security enforcement and was one of the main men that built the small living complexes.

"We'll go somewhere else one day," Ross would say. Dawson was still waiting. He figured by now it wasn't going to happen, because with each passing year, Ross had even more responsibility.

Every civilization, at least the functioning ones, were so far apart and separated by the new lakes, the only way there was by boat. It took a lot of bartering to even get passage.

North of the Rockies, there was a lot of area not flooded, but the land was overrun with Trancers, there were more of them than people who were normal. Everyone kept saying they'd die out, but they never did.

Dawson fully believed they were the new evolution of man.

Ross told him it was nonsense.

Life was simple. He got up, went to school and then work. At fifteen he had a job, everyone over the age of thirteen did. He worked in pickling and hated it. Leadville Nine was the smallest of the twelve complexes. A hundred and thirteen people lived there. They farmed their own section and bartered with neighboring villages.

When he was younger he used to think that Ross and Morgan would end up together. They never got along, they always fought. Dawson remembered how she used to be. She ended up being pretty nice. She married a guy in Leadville Seven and had two kids. He visited her every week.

Sister Helena was the one only one who left the mountain and was teaching in California somewhere. She took a boat and only came back three times in the past seven years.

He missed her, he thought of her, but rarely saw her. That was life now.

"Hey." Ross snapped his finger. "Are you listening?"

"I almost have this," Dawson said. "I really do."

"I know, but your hair is too long. It needs to be cut. I want to spend time with you. Hang out. Can you please put down the guitar? I know it's hard to do, it's like an extension of your body."

Dawson laughed. "Alright He grabbed a cloth, wiped off the neck of the guitar to free it from smudges, then gently set it on his bed. The guitar meant a lot to Dawson. It hadn't left his side since it left Judd's hands.

"Can you clean up this mess later?" Ross asked.

"Aw, man, you kill me." Dawson groaned.

"No, you … kill me." Ross mussed his shaggy hair. "Let's go. We won't be long."

Dawson nodded as he reached down and closed his notebook.

"You writing a new song?" Ross asked.

"Yeah, I am. Trying to anyways."

"Can I hear it?"

"When we get back." Dawson followed him through the door.

"What's it called?"

"It's called …. Call me Mr. Heston."

Closed mouth, Ross nodded. "Good title."

"Yeah. Yeah it is."

The title was good and had more meaning than Ross probably would understand.

Life wasn't all that exciting for Dawson, however it was good in its own way. He had his music, he had Ross, and he had his memories.

In a world that was tossed upside down, Dawson had landed on his feet.

Before leaving with Ross, Dawson looked back once at the guitar on his bed and pulled the door closed with a smile.

<><><><>

Thank you so much for diving into this book. I hope you enjoyed it.

Please visit my website www.jacquelinedruga.com and sign up for my mailing list for updates, freebies, new releases and giveaways. And, don't forget my new Kindle club!

Your support is invaluable to me. I welcome and respond to your feedback. Please feel free to email me at Jacqueline@jacquelinedruga.com

Printed in Great Britain
by Amazon